Ford Madox Ford

The Queen Who Flew

.

Ford Madox Ford

The Queen Who Flew

ISBN/EAN: 9783337322830

Printed in Europe, USA, Canada, Australia, Japan

Cover: Foto ©Andreas Hilbeck / pixelio.de

More available books at **www.hansebooks.com**

The Queen

Who Flew

The Queen

A Fairy Tale

Who Flew

BY

FORD HUFFER

AUTHOR OF "THE BROWN OWL"
"SHIFTING OF THE FIRE," ETC.

With a Frontispiece by
SIR E. BURNE JONES

AND

Border Design by
C. R. B. BARRETT

LONDON
BLISS, SANDS & FOSTER
CRAVEN STREET, STRAND, W.C.
1894

TO

A PRINCESS OF THE OLD TIME
BEFORE US

THIS TALE

IS DUE AND DEDICATED.

———◆———

Over the leas the Princess came,
On the sward of the cliffs that breast the sea,
With her cheeks aglow and her hair a flame,
That seared the eyes and blinded them,
And now is but a memory.

Over the leas, the wind-tossed dream,
Over the leas above the sea,
Passed and went to reign supreme.
—No need of a crown or diadem
In the kingdom of misty Memory.

THE QUEEN WHO FLEW.

ONCE upon a time a Queen sat in her garden.
She was quite a young, young Queen; but
that was a long while ago, so she would be older
now. But, for all she was Queen over a great and
powerful country, she led a very quiet life, and sat
a great deal alone in her garden watching the roses
grow, and talking to a bat that hung, head downwards, with its wings folded, for all the world like
an umbrella, beneath the shade of a rose tree overhanging her favourite marble seat. She did not
know much about the bat, not even that it could
fly, for her servants and nurses would never allow
her to be out at dusk, and the bat was a great deal
too weak-eyed to fly about in the broad daylight.

B

But, one summer day, it happened that there was a revolution in the land, and the Queen's servants, not knowing who was likely to get the upper hand, left the Queen all alone, and went to look at the fight that was raging.

But you must understand that in those days a revolution was a thing very different from what it would be to-day.

Instead of trying to get rid of the Queen altogether, the great nobles of the kingdom merely fought violently with each other for possession of the Queen's person. Then they would proclaim themselves Regents of the kingdom and would issue bills of attainder against all their rivals, saying they were traitors against the Queen's Government.

In fact, a revolution in those days was like what is called a change of Ministry now, save for the fact that they were rather fond of indulging themselves by decapitating their rivals when they had the chance, which of course one would never think of doing nowadays.

The Queen and the bat had been talking a good

deal that afternoon—about the weather and about the revolution and the colour of cats and the like.

"The raven will have a good time of it for a day or two," the bat said.

But the Queen shuddered. "Don't be horrid," she said.

"I wonder who'll get the upper hand?" the bat said.

"I'm sure I don't care a bit," the Queen retorted. "It doesn't make any difference to me. They all give me things to sign, and they all say I'm very beautiful."

"That's because they want to marry you," the bat said.

And the Queen answered, "I suppose it is; but I shan't marry them. And I wish *all* my attendants weren't deaf and dumb; it makes it so awfully dull for me."

"That's so that they shan't abuse the Regent behind his back," the bat said. "Well, I shall take a fly." The truth was, he felt insulted that the Queen should say she was dull when she had him to talk to.

But the Queen was quite frightened when he whizzed past her head and out into the dusky evening, where she could see him flitting about jerkily, and squeaking shrilly to paralyse the flies with fright.

After a while he got over his fit of sulks, and came back again to hang in his accustomed bough.

"Why—you can fly!" the Queen said breathlessly. It gave her a new idea of the importance of the bat.

The bat said, "I can." He was flattered by her admiration.

"I wish *I* could fly," the Queen said. "It would be so much more exciting than being boxed up here."

The bat said, "Why don't you?"

"Because I haven't got wings, I suppose," the Queen said.

"You shouldn't suppose," the bat said sharply. "Half the evils in the world come from people supposing."

"What are the 'evils in the world'?" the Queen said.

And the bat answered, " What I don't you even know that, y u ignorant little thing? The evils in the world are ever so many—strong winds so that one can't fly straight, and cold weather so that the flies die, and rheumatic pains in one's wing-joints, and cats and swallows."

" I like cats," the Queen said; "and swallows are very pretty."

"That's what *you* think," the bat said angrily. " But you're nobody. Now, I hate cats because they always want to eat me; and I hate swallows because they always eat what I want to eat—flies. They are the real evils of the world."

The Queen saw that he was angry, and she held her peace for a while.

" I'm not nobody, all the same," she thought to herself. " I'm the Queen of the 'most prosperous and contented nation in the world,' though I don't quite understand what it means. But it will never do to offend the bat, it is so dreadfully dull when he won't talk ; " so she said, " Would it be possible for me to fly ?" for a great longing had come into her heart to be able to fly

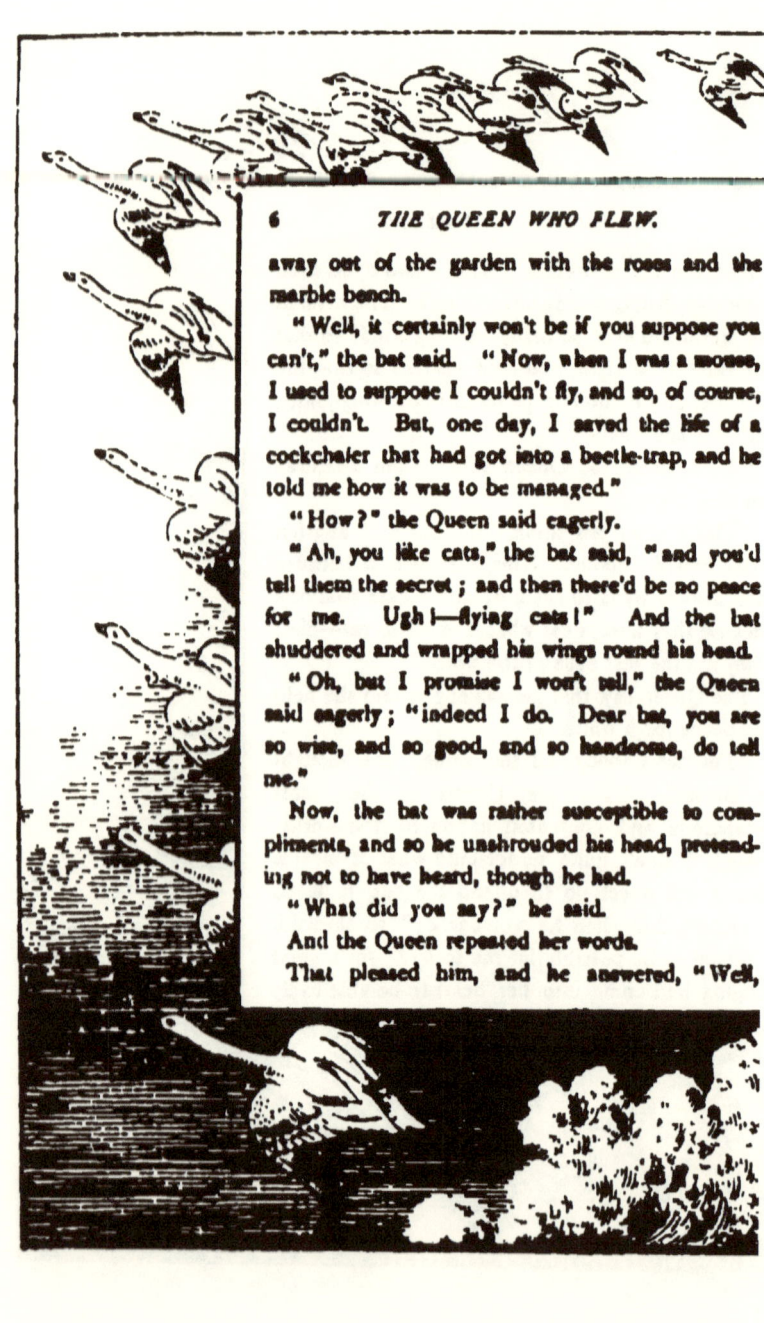

away out of the garden with the roses and the marble bench.

"Well, it certainly won't be if you suppose you can't," the bat said. "Now, when I was a mouse, I used to suppose I couldn't fly, and so, of course, I couldn't. But, one day, I saved the life of a cockchafer that had got into a beetle-trap, and he told me how it was to be managed."

"How?" the Queen said eagerly.

"Ah, you like cats," the bat said, "and you'd tell them the secret; and then there'd be no peace for me. Ugh!—flying cats!" And the bat shuddered and wrapped his wings round his head.

"Oh, but I promise I won't tell," the Queen said eagerly; "indeed I do. Dear bat, you are so wise, and so good, and so handsome, do tell me."

Now, the bat was rather susceptible to compliments, and so he unshrouded his head, pretending not to have heard, though he had.

"What did you say?" he said.

And the Queen repeated her words.

That pleased him, and he answered, "Well,

there's a certain flower that has two remarkable properties—one, that people who carry it about with them can always fly, and the other, that it will restore the blind to sight."

·" Yes ; but I shall have to travel over ever so many mountains and rivers and things before I can find it," the Queen said dismally.

" How do you know that ? " the bat asked sharply.

" I don't know it, I only supposed it ; at least I've read it in books."

· " Well, of course, if you go supposing things and reading them in books, I can't do anything for you," the bat said. " 'The only good I can see in books is that they breed bookworms, and the worms turn into flies ; but even they aren't very good to eat. When I was a mouse, though, I used to nibble books to pieces, and the bits made rare good nests. So there is *some* good in the most useless of things. But I don't need a nest now that I can fly."

" How did you come to be able to fly ? " the Queen asked.

"Well, after what the cockchafer told me, I just ran out into the garden, and when I found the flower, as I hadn't any pocket to put it in so as to have it always by me, I just ate it up, and from that time forward I have been able to fly ever so well."

The Queen said, "Oh, how nice! And is the flower actually here in the garden? Tell me which it is, please do."

"Well, I'll tell you if you'll bring me a nice piece of raw meat, and a little red flannel for my rheumatism."

Just at that moment the sound of a great bell sounded out into the garden.

"Oh, how annoying!" the Queen said. "Just as it was beginning to be interesting! Now I shall have to go in to dinner. But I'll bring you the meat and the flannel to-morrow, and then you'll tell me, won't you?"

The bat said, "We'll see about it," and so the Queen arose from her seat, and, stooping to avoid the roses that caught at her, went out towards the palace and up the marble steps into it.

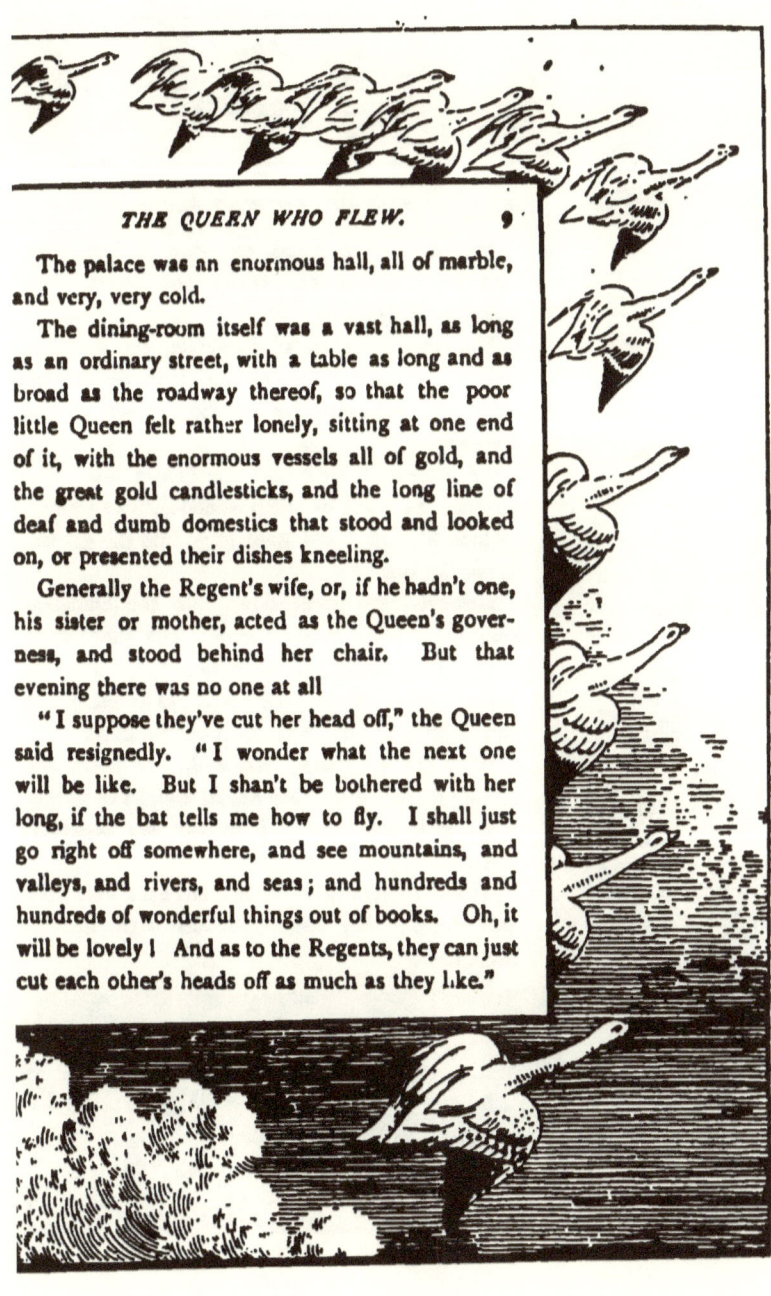

The palace was an enormous hall, all of marble, and very, very cold.

The dining-room itself was a vast hall, as long as an ordinary street, with a table as long and as broad as the roadway thereof, so that the poor little Queen felt rather lonely, sitting at one end of it, with the enormous vessels all of gold, and the great gold candlesticks, and the long line of deaf and dumb domestics that stood and looked on, or presented their dishes kneeling.

Generally the Regent's wife, or, if he hadn't one, his sister or mother, acted as the Queen's governess, and stood behind her chair. But that evening there was no one at all

"I suppose they've cut her head off," the Queen said resignedly. "I wonder what the next one will be like. But I shan't be bothered with her long, if the bat tells me how to fly. I shall just go right off somewhere, and see mountains, and valleys, and rivers, and seas; and hundreds and hundreds of wonderful things out of books. Oh, it will be lovely! And as to the Regents, they can just cut each other's heads off as much as they like."

And so, having dined, she went to bed, and lay a long time awake thinking how delightful it would be to fly.

The next morning, at breakfast, she found a note to say that the Lord Blackjowl desired an early audience with her on the subject of the Regency.

"I suppose I *must* go," the Queen said. "I do hope he won't be much wounded, it's so nasty to look at, and I *did* want to go into the garden to see the bat."

However, she went down into the audience chamber at once, to get it over. The guard drew back the curtain in the doorway and she went in. A great man with a black beard was awaiting her, and at her entrance sank down on one knee.

"Oh, get up, please," she said. "I don't like talking to men when they kneel, it looks so stupid. What is it you want? I suppose it's about the Regency."

The Lord Blackjowl arose. His eyes were little and sharp; they seemed to look right through the Queen.

"Your Majesty is correct, as so peerless a lady must be," he said. "The nobles and people were groaning under the yoke of the late traitor and tyrant who called himself Regent, and so we took the liberty, the great liberty, of—— "

"Oh yes, I know what you want," the Queen interrupted him. "You want to be pardoned for the unconstitutionality of it. So I suppose I shall have to pardon you. If you give me the paper I'll sign it."

The Lord Blackjowl handed her one of many papers that he held in his hand.

"If your Majesty will be graciously pleased to sign it here."

So the Queen sat down at a table and signed the crackling paper "Eldrida—Queen."

"I never sign it 'Eldrida R.,'" she said. "It's ridiculous to sign it in a language that isn't one's own. Now I suppose you want me to sign a paper appointing you Regent?"

The Lord Blackjowl looked at her from under his shaggy eyebrows.

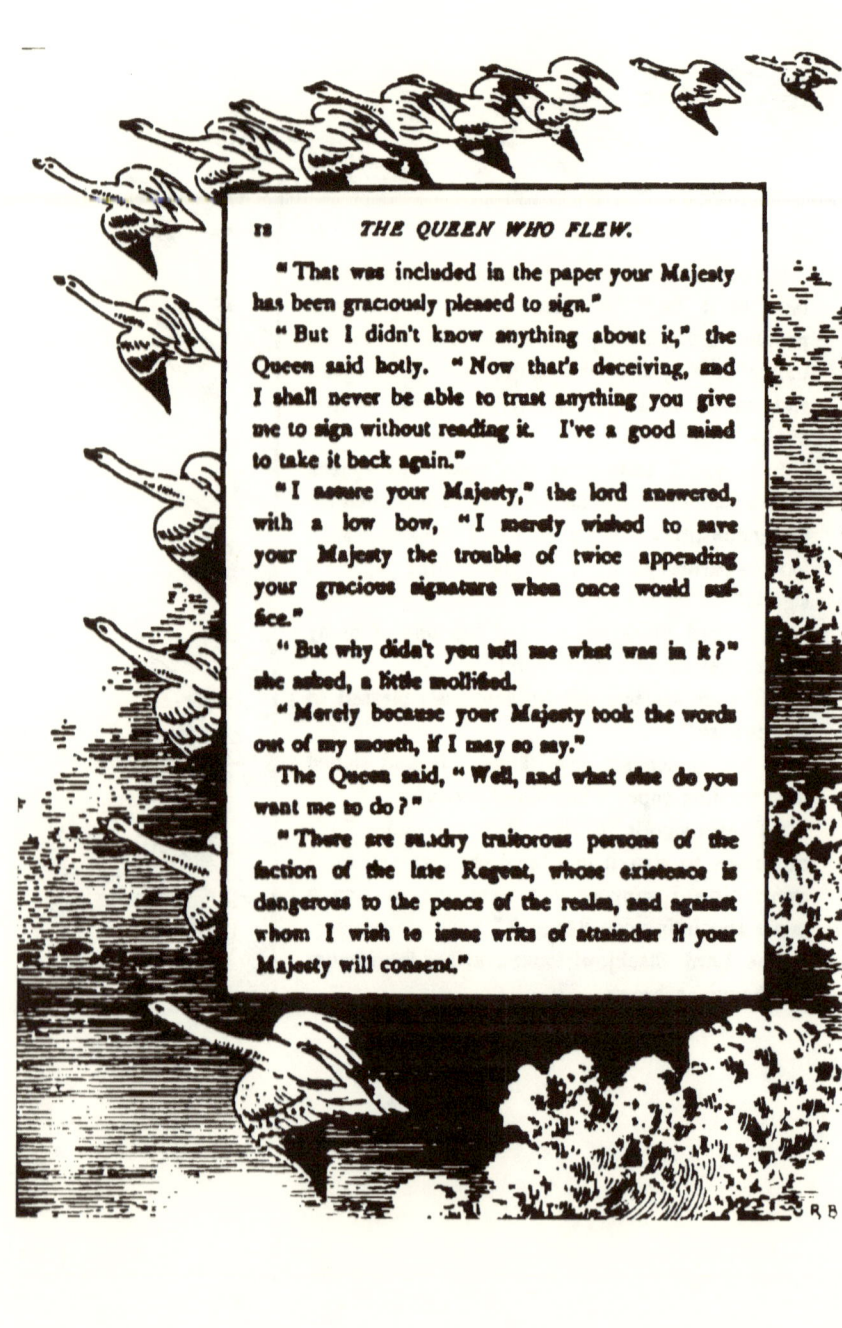

"That was included in the paper your Majesty has been graciously pleased to sign."

"But I didn't know anything about it," the Queen said hotly. "Now that's deceiving, and I shall never be able to trust anything you give me to sign without reading it. I've a good mind to take it back again."

"I assure your Majesty," the lord answered, with a low bow, "I merely wished to save your Majesty the trouble of twice appending your gracious signature when once would suffice."

"But why didn't you tell me what was in it?" she asked, a little mollified.

"Merely because your Majesty took the words out of my mouth, if I may so say."

The Queen said, "Well, and what else do you want me to do?"

"There are sundry traitorous persons of the faction of the late Regent, whose existence is dangerous to the peace of the realm, and against whom I wish to issue writs of attainder if your Majesty will consent."

"Yes, I thought so," the Queen said. "How many are there?"

"Three thousand nine hundred and forty," the Regent said, looking at a great scroll.

"Good gracious!" the Queen said. "Why, that's five times as many as ever there were before."

The Regent stroked his beard. "There is a great deal of disaffection in the land," he said.

"Why, the last Regent said the people were ever so contented," the Queen answered.

"The last Regent has deceived your Majesty."

"That's what they all say about the last Regent. Why, it was only the other day that he told me that you were deceitful—and you *are*—and he said that you had thrown your wife into a yard full of hungry dogs, in order that you might marry me."

"Your Majesty," the Regent said, flushing with heavy anger, "the late Regent was a tyrant, and all tyrants are untruthful, as your Majesty's wisdom must tell you. My wife had the misfortune to fall into a bear-pit, and, as for my

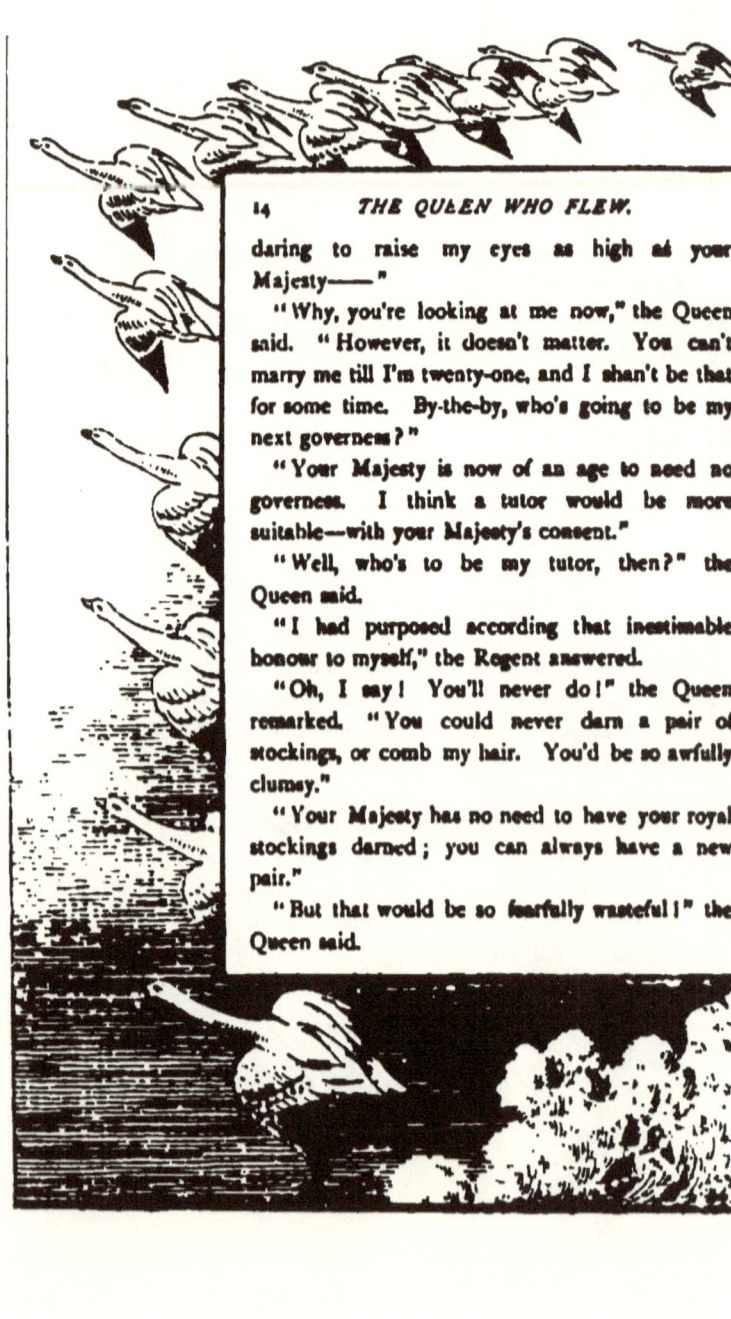

daring to raise my eyes as high as your
Majesty——"

"Why, you're looking at me now," the Queen
said. "However, it doesn't matter. You can't
marry me till I'm twenty-one, and I shan't be that
for some time. By-the-by, who's going to be my
next governess?"

"Your Majesty is now of an age to need no
governess. I think a tutor would be more
suitable—with your Majesty's consent."

"Well, who's to be my tutor, then?" the
Queen said.

"I had purposed according that inestimable
honour to myself," the Regent answered.

"Oh, I say! You'll never do!" the Queen
remarked. "You could never darn a pair of
stockings, or comb my hair. You'd be so awfully
clumsy."

"Your Majesty has no need to have your royal
stockings darned; you can always have a new
pair."

"But that would be so fearfully wasteful!" the
Queen said.

" Your Majesty might give the other pairs to the poor."

" But what *are* ' the poor ' ? "

" The poor are wicked, idle people—too wicked to work and earn the money, and too dirty to wear stockings," the Regent said.

" But what would be the good of my stockings to them ? " the Queen asked.

"It is the usual thing, your Majesty," the Regent said. " But will your Majesty be pleased to sign these papers ? "

The Queen said, " Oh yes, I'll sign them, if you'll just go down into the kitchen and ask for a piece of raw meat, about the size of my hand, and a piece of red flannel about large enough to go round a bat. Oh, and what's a good thing for rheumatism ? "

The Regent looked a little surprised. " I — your Majesty, I really don't exactly know."

" Oh, well, ask the cook or somebody."

" Well, but—couldn't I send a servant, your Majesty ? " the Regent said.

" No, that wouldn't be any good," the Queen

said. "If you're to take the place of my governess you'll have to do that sort of thing, you know."

The Regent bowed. "Of course I shall be only too grateful for your Majesty's commands. I merely thought that your Majesty might need some assistance in signing the papers."

But the Queen answered, "Oh no, I can manage that sort of thing well enough myself. I'm quite used to it; so be quick, and remember, a nice juicy piece of raw meat and some red flannel, and—oh, opodeldoc; that's just the thing. Be quick! I don't want to keep the bat waiting."

The Regent went backwards out of the room, bowing at every three steps, and, as he was clad in armour from top to toe, he made a clanking noise —quite like a tinker's cart, if you've ever heard one.

So, left to herself, the Queen signed the papers one after the other. They all began—

"BY THE QUEEN, A PROCLAMATION,
E.R.

"*Whereas by Our Proclamation given this 1st day of May——*

But the Queen never read any further than that, because she could never quite understand what it all meant. At the last signature she happened to make a little blot, and somehow or other the ink happened to get into one of her nails, and that annoyed her. It *is* so difficult to get ink out of one's nails.

"I don't care if I never sign another Proclamation," she said; "and I hope I never shall. Now, look here,".she continued to the Regent, who at that moment entered. "If you were a governess I should be able to make you get this ink out; but how can I ask a man to do that?"

"I will make the attempt, if your Majesty pleases," the Regent said.

"Well, but you haven't got any nail-scissors," the Queen replied.

"I might use my sword," the Regent suggested.

But the Queen shivered. "Ugh! fancy having a great ugly thing like that for it!" she said. "Oh, well, you've brought the things! Here are your papers. They're all signed; and, if you

c

want anything else, you'll have to come into the garden."

And she took up the meat and the flannel and the opodeldoc and went into the garden, leaving the Regent with the idea that he had made rather a bad business by becoming the Queen's attendant. But he was a very determined man, and merely set his teeth the firmer.

Under the overhanging rose tree the Queen sat awaiting the bat's awakening.

"It never does to wake him up," she said. "It makes him so bad tempered."

So she sat patiently and watched the rose-petals that every now and then fluttered down on the wind.

It was well on towards the afternoon, after the Queen had had her dinner, before he awoke.

"Oh, you're there?" he said. He had made the same remark every day for the last two years —which made seven hundred and thirty-one times, one of the years having been leap-year.

The Queen said, "Yes, here I am!"

The bat yawned. "What's the weather like?" he asked.

The Queen answered, "Oh, it's very nice, and you promised to tell me the flower that would make me fly."

"I shan't," the bat said. "You'd eat up all the flies—a great thing like you."

The Queen's eyes filled with tears, it was so disappointing.

"Oh, I promise I won't eat *any* flies," she said; "and I'll go right away and leave you in peace."

The bat said, "Um! there's something in that."

"And look," the Queen continued, "I've brought you your meat and flannel, and some stuff that's good for rheumatism."

The bat's eyes twinkled with delight. "Well, I'll tell you," he said. "Only you must promise, first, that you won't tell any one the secret; and secondly, that you won't eat any flies."

"Oh yes, I'll promise that willingly enough."

"Well, put the things up here on the top of the seat and I'll tell you."

The Queen did as she was bidden, and the bat continued—

"The flower you want is at this moment being trodden on by your foot."

The Queen felt a little startled, but, looking down, saw a delicate white flower that had trailed from a border and was being crushed beneath her small green shoes.

"What! the wind-flower?" she said. "I always thought it was only a weed."

"You shouldn't think," the bat said. "It's as bad as supposing."

"Well, and how am I to set about flying?" the Queen asked.

And the bat answered sharply, "Why, fly. Put the flower somewhere about you, and then go off. Only be careful not to knock against things."

The Queen thought for a moment, and then plucked a handful and a handful and yet a handful of the wind-flowers, and, having twined them into a carcanet, wound them into her soft gold-brown hair, beneath her small crown royal.

"Good-bye, dear bat," she said. She had grown to like the bat, for all his strange appearance and surly speeches.

The bat remarked, "Good riddance." He was always a little irritable just after awakening.

So the Queen went out from under the arbour, and made a first essay at flying.

"I'll make just a short flight at first," she said, and gave a little jump, and in a moment she flew right over a rose bush and came down softly on the turf on its further side, quite like a not too timid pigeon that has to make a little flight from before a horse's feet.

"Oh, come, that was a success," she said to herself. "And it really is true. Well, I'll just practise a little before I start to see the world."

So she flew over several trees, gradually going higher and higher, until at last she caught a glimpse of the red town roofs, and then, in a swift moment's rush, she flew over the high white wall and alighted in the road that bordered it.

"Hullo!" a voice said before she had got used to the new sensation of being out in the world. "Hullo! where did you drop from?"

"I didn't drop—I flew," the Queen said severely; and she looked at the man.

He was stretched on the ground, leaning his back against the wall, and basking in the hot sunlight that fell on him. He was very ragged and very dirty, and he had neither shoes nor stockings. By his side was a basket in which, over white paper frills, nodded the heads of young ferns.

"Why, who are you?" the Queen said. And then her eyes fell on his bare feet. They reminded her of what the Regent had said that morning. "Oh, you must be the poor," she said, "and you want my stockings."

"I don't know about your stockings, lady," the man said; "but if you've got any old clothes to spare, I could give you some nice pots of flowers for them."

The Queen said, "Why, what good would that do you?"

And the man answered, "I should sell them and get some money. I'm fearfully hungry."

"Why don't you have something to eat, then?" the Queen said.

And the man replied, "Because I haven't got any money to buy it with."

"Why don't you take it, then?"

"Because it would be stealing, and stealing's wicked; besides, I should be sent to prison for it."

"I don't understand quite what you mean," the Queen said. "But come with me somewhere where we can get some food, and you shall have as much as you like."

The fern-seller arose with alacrity.

"There's a shop near here where they sell some delicious honey-cakes."

"I can't make it out," the Queen said to herself. "If he's hungry he can't be contented; and yet the Regent said every one was contented in the land, because of his being Regent. He must have been mistaken, or else this man must be one of the traitors."

And aloud she said, "Is there a bill of attainder out against you?"

The beggar shook his head. "I guess not," he said. "Tradesmen won't let the likes of me run up bills."

It was a remark the Queen could not understand

at all. They crossed the market-place that lay before the palace door.

"There's no market to-day because the people are all afraid the revolution isn't over yet."

"Oh, but it is," the Queen said; "I made the Lord Blackjowl Regent to-day."

The beggar looked at her with a strange expression; but the Queen continued—

"I don't see what harm the revolution could do to the market."

"Why, don't you see," the beggar said, "when they get to fighting the arrows fly about all over the place, and the horses would knock the stalls over. Besides, the soldiers steal everything, or set fire to it. Look, there's a house still smouldering."

And, indeed, one of the market houses was a heap of charred ruins.

"But what was the good of it?" the Queen asked.

And the beggar answered, "Well, you see, it belonged to one of the opposite party, and he wouldn't surrender and have his head chopped off."

" I should think not," the Queen said.

The streets were quite empty, and all the shutters were closed. Here and there an arrow was sticking into the walls or the doors.

" Do people never walk about the streets ? " the Queen asked.

" It wouldn't be safe when there's a revolution on," the beggar answered.

Just at that moment they arrived before the door of a house that, like all the rest, was closely shut up. Over the door was written—

"JAMES GRUB,
Honey-cake Maker."

Here the beggar stopped and began to beat violently at the door with his staff.

The sound of the blows echoed along the streets, —and then from within came dismal shouts of " Murder ! " " Police ! " " Fire ! "

But the beggar called back, "Nonsense, James Grubb; it's only a lady come for some honey-cakes."

Then, after a long while, there was a clatter of

chains behind the door, and it was opened just an inch, so that the Queen could see an old man's face peeping cautiously out at her. The sight seemed to reassure him, for he opened the door and bobbed nervously. At other times he would have bowed suavely.

"Will your ladyship be pleased to enter?" he said. "I want to shut the door; it is so dangerous to have it open with all these revolutions about."

The Queen complied with his request, and found herself in a little dark shop, only lighted dimly through the round air-holes in the shutters.

"Give this man some honey-cakes," she said; and the honey-cake maker seemed only too delighted.

"How many shall I give him, madam?" he said.

"As many as he wants, of course," the Queen answered sharply.

The beggar proceeded to help himself, and made a clean sweep of all the cakes that were on the counter. There was a big hole in his coat, and

into that he thrust them, so that the lining at last was quite full.

The honey-cake maker was extremely pleased at the sight, for he had not expected to sell any cakes that day.

When the cakes had all disappeared there was an awkward pause.

"Now I'll go on again," the Queen said.

"But you haven't paid," the honey-cake maker said in some alarm.

"Pay !" said the Queen. "What do you mean?"

"Paid for the cakes, I mean," the honey-cake maker said.

"I don't understand you," she answered. "I am the Queen; I never pay for what I eat."

"She *is* the Queen," the beggar said; "and if you don't take care she'll have your head off."

The honey-cake maker jumped back so suddenly that he sat down in a tub of honey and stuck there doubled up with his knees to his chin.

"O Lord ! O Lord !" he said. "What shall I do? what shall I do?—all my cakes gone, and never to be paid !"

"You won't want to be paid if your head's cut off," the beggar said.

But the Queen answered, "Nonsense. No one's going to cut your head off; and I dare say, if you ask them at the palace, they'll pay you, whatever it means. Just pull him out of the tub," she continued to the beggar, for the unfortunate honey-baker, not being able to move, remained gasping in the tub.

So the beggar pulled him out, and, for all his fright, his business spirit did not desert him.

"Will your Majesty deign to sign an order for payment?" he said.

And the Queen answered, "Good gracious, no, I won't; the ink always gets into my finger-nails."

The honey-cake maker bowed lower still. "At least, your Majesty, deign to give me your signet-ring as a token."

"Oh, I'll give you that," the Queen said; and she drew it from her finger.

The honey-cake maker suddenly smote his fore-head with his hand, as though an idea had struck him.

along the passage wall.

The beggar did as he was asked, and placed it against the house.

"Whatever is he going to do now?" the Queen thought to herself, and, being in the street, awaited the turn of events.

Presently the honey-cake maker came out, carrying a pail of black paint and a large brush, and, thus equipped, ascended the ladder and began to paint, under the

"JAMES GRUBB,
Honey-cake Maker,"
"to Her Majesty the Queen and the R——"

But he had got no further than that, when, with tumultuous shouts, a body of soldiers came rushing round a corner, and, seeing the honey-cake maker on the ladder and his door open, they at once tumbled pell-mell into the shop.

No sooner did the unfortunate maker of cakes see this, than, in his haste to descend the ladder,

his foot slipped, and he came to the ground, with the paint out of the pot running dismally all over his head.

"Oh dear! oh dear!" the Queen said, and went to pick him up, when, at that moment, the soldiers having found nothing in the shop but a tub of honey and a tub of flour, came out again, not quite as fast as they had entered, until they saw the Queen, when they at once rushed to surround her, and one of them caught at her crown, and another at her bracelets, and another at her lace-handkerchief.

The Queen said, "Leave me alone, do you hear?"

But the soldiers answered, "In the Queen's name, surrender."

"Well, I shouldn't surrender in any name but my own, and I shan't surrender at all. I am the Queen."

Whereupon the leader of the soldiers, who had not had the fortune to get at any of the Queen's jewellery, said, "Release the lady;" and, rather crestfallen, the soldiers obeyed him.

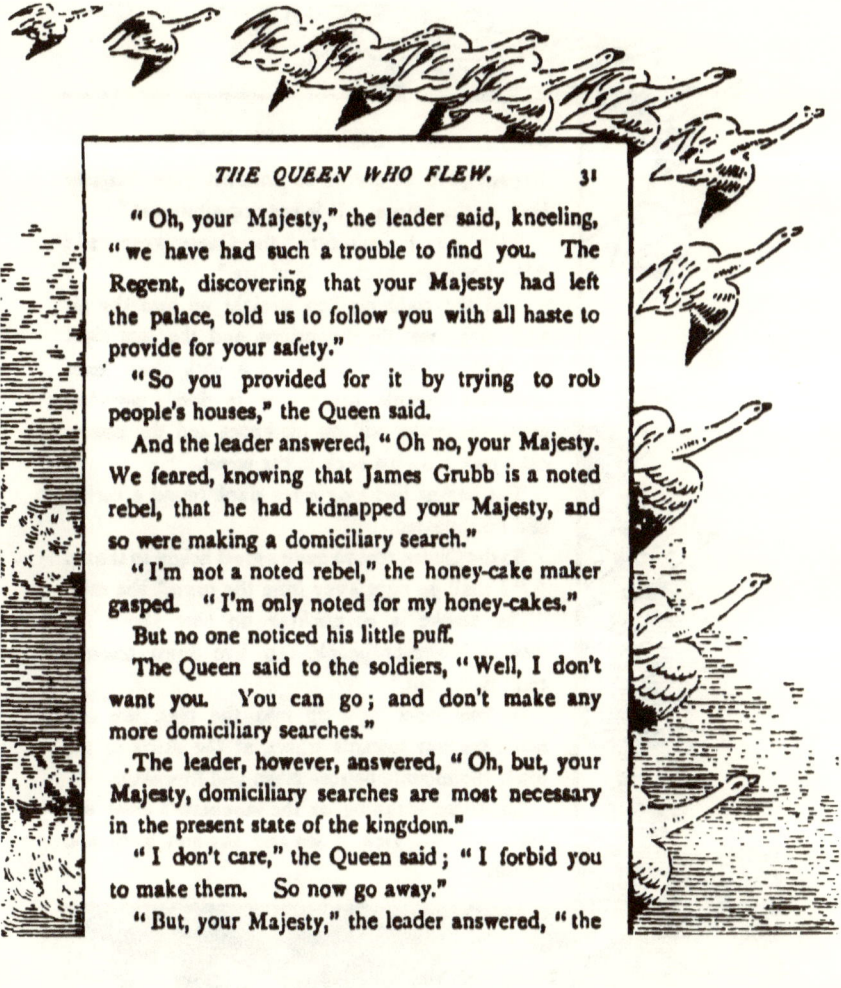

"Oh, your Majesty," the leader said, kneeling, "we have had such a trouble to find you. The Regent, discovering that your Majesty had left the palace, told us to follow you with all haste to provide for your safety."

"So you provided for it by trying to rob people's houses," the Queen said.

And the leader answered, "Oh no, your Majesty. We feared, knowing that James Grubb is a noted rebel, that he had kidnapped your Majesty, and so were making a domiciliary search."

"I'm not a noted rebel," the honey-cake maker gasped. "I'm only noted for my honey-cakes."

But no one noticed his little puff.

The Queen said to the soldiers, "Well, I don't want you. You can go; and don't make any more domiciliary searches."

The leader, however, answered, "Oh, but, your Majesty, domiciliary searches are most necessary in the present state of the kingdom."

"I don't care," the Queen said; "I forbid you to make them. So now go away."

"But, your Majesty," the leader answered, "the

Regent gave us orders to conduct your Majesty back to the palace.   It is not constitutional."

"I'm sure I don't care," the Queen answered; "I'm not going back.   Good-bye."

And she suddenly flew straight up into the air and away over the housetops, and the last sight she had of them showed them, with their faces upturned towards her, gazing in dumb astonishment, the leader still on his knees and the honey-cake maker on his back in the street.

The beggar had long since slunk round a corner and disappeared.

So the Queen rose to quite a great height in the air.

"I shall go right away from the town," she said. "The smoke is so choking up here above the roofs.   However people can live down there I can't make out."

So she went right up into the blue sky and made her way towards where, at the skirts of the town, the mountains rose steep and frowning.

Up there, standing on the mountain's crest, she had a glorious view of sea and sky and town and country.

The sea threw back the deep blue of the sky above, and the white wave-horses flecked its surface, and the ships passed silently far out at sea; down below her feet, it beat against the rocky base of the cliff, and in and out amongst the spray the seagulls flew like a white cloud.

The town lay in a narrow valley, broad at the sea face, and running inwards into narrowness between grey, grand hills, right to where it disappeared in the windings of the pass. Down below, in the harbour, she could see the boats getting ready for sea.

"Oh, how wonderful!" the Queen said; "and it all belongs to me—at least, so they say—though I can't quite see what good it does me, for I can't be everywhere at once. And I can't even make the hills move or the sea heave its breast; so that I can't see that it does me any more good than any one else, because it isn't even constitutional for me to be here. I ought to be down there in the palace garden, seeing nothing at all. However, it's very lovely here, so I mustn't grumble. I wonder how the bat is getting on, and the Regent, and all."

D

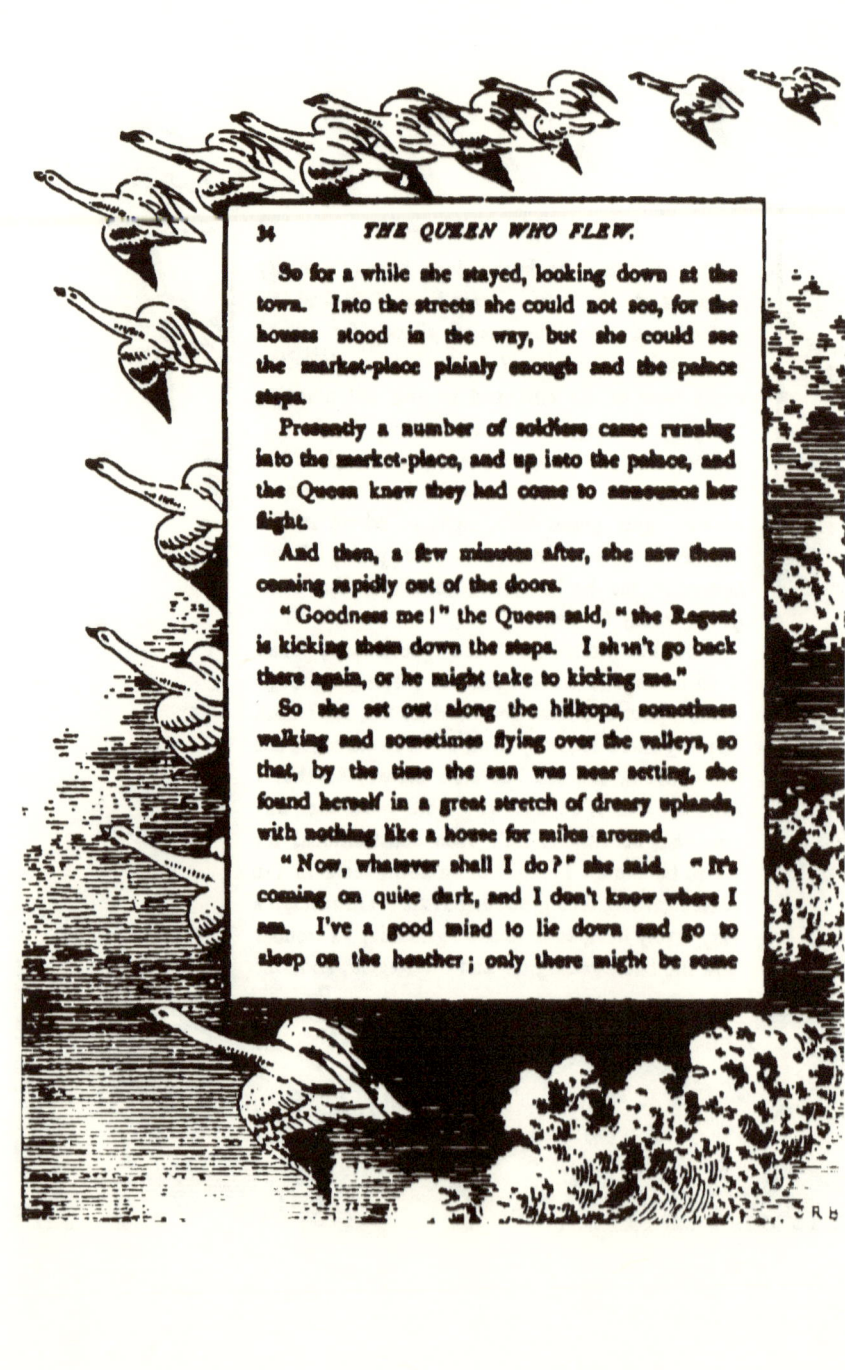

So for a while she stayed, looking down at the town. Into the streets she could not see, for the houses stood in the way, but she could see the market-place plainly enough and the palace steps.

Presently a number of soldiers came running into the market-place, and up into the palace, and the Queen knew they had come to announce her flight.

And then, a few minutes after, she saw them coming rapidly out of the doors.

"Goodness me!" the Queen said, "the Regent is kicking them down the steps. I shan't go back there again, or he might take to kicking me."

So she set out along the hilltops, sometimes walking and sometimes flying over the valleys, so that, by the time the sun was near setting, she found herself in a great stretch of dreary uplands, with nothing like a house for miles around.

"Now, whatever shall I do?" she said. "It's coming on quite dark, and I don't know where I am. I've a good mind to lie down and go to sleep on the heather; only there might be some

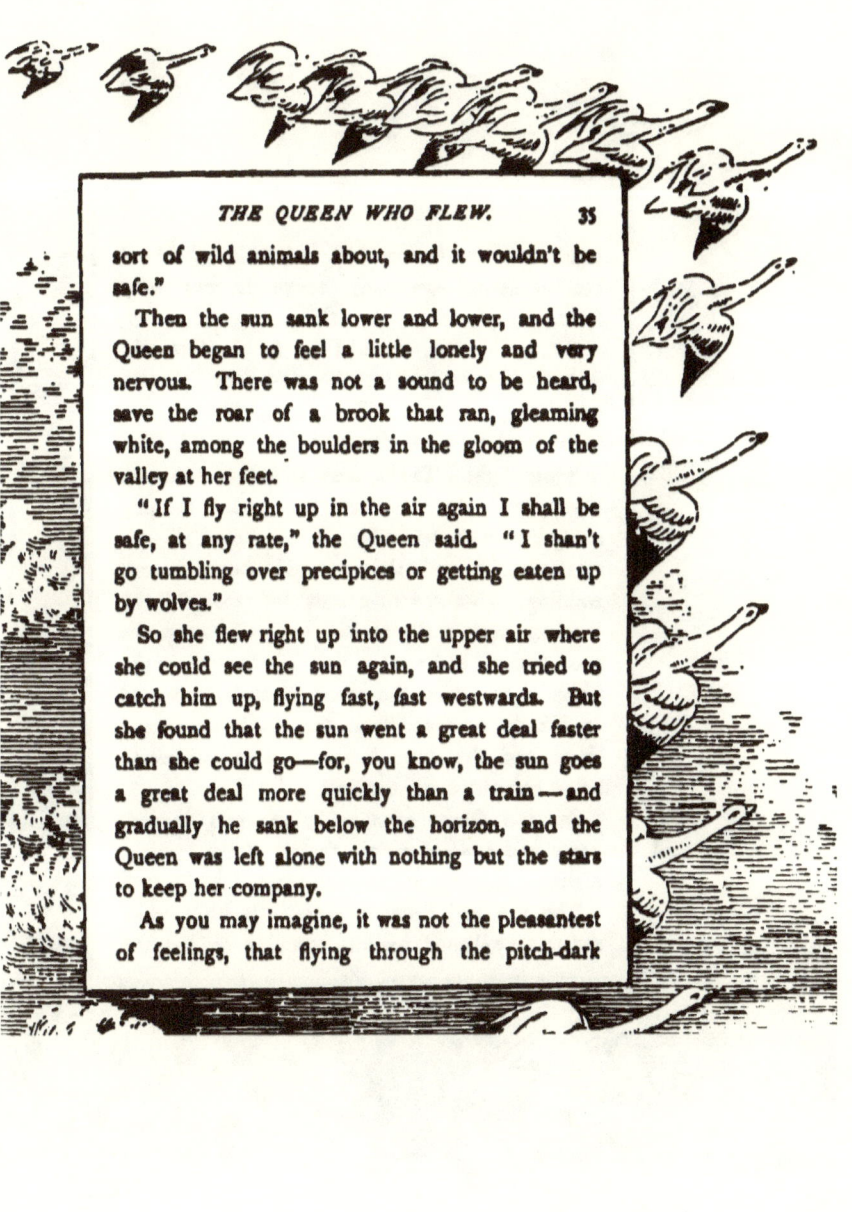

sort of wild animals about, and it wouldn't be safe."

Then the sun sank lower and lower, and the Queen began to feel a little lonely and very nervous. There was not a sound to be heard, save the roar of a brook that ran, gleaming white, among the boulders in the gloom of the valley at her feet.

"If I fly right up in the air again I shall be safe, at any rate," the Queen said. "I shan't go tumbling over precipices or getting eaten up by wolves."

So she flew right up into the upper air where she could see the sun again, and she tried to catch him up, flying fast, fast westwards. But she found that the sun went a great deal faster than she could go—for, you know, the sun goes a great deal more quickly than a train—and gradually he sank below the horizon, and the Queen was left alone with nothing but the stars to keep her company.

As you may imagine, it was not the pleasantest of feelings, that flying through the pitch-dark

night, and the Queen felt continually afraid of
running against something, though she was really
far too high to do any such thing.

But, for all that, she had the dread constantly
in her mind, until at last the moon crept silently
into being above a hill, seeming like an old
friend, and soon all the land below was bathed
in white light. The Queen glided on; like a
black cloud, she could see her shadow running
along the fields below her. She watched till she
grew sleepier and sleepier, and found herself
nodding, to wake with a start and then fall off
to sleep again; till, at last, she fell asleep for
good and all, and went sailing quietly along in the
white night, whilst the moon gradually mounted
up straight overhead, and then sank lower and
lower, and the dawn began to wash the world
below her with a warmer light.

But the Queen slept softly on; and, indeed,
never bed was softer than the air of the summer
night.

The sun had been up some little while when
she was awakened by just touching on the top

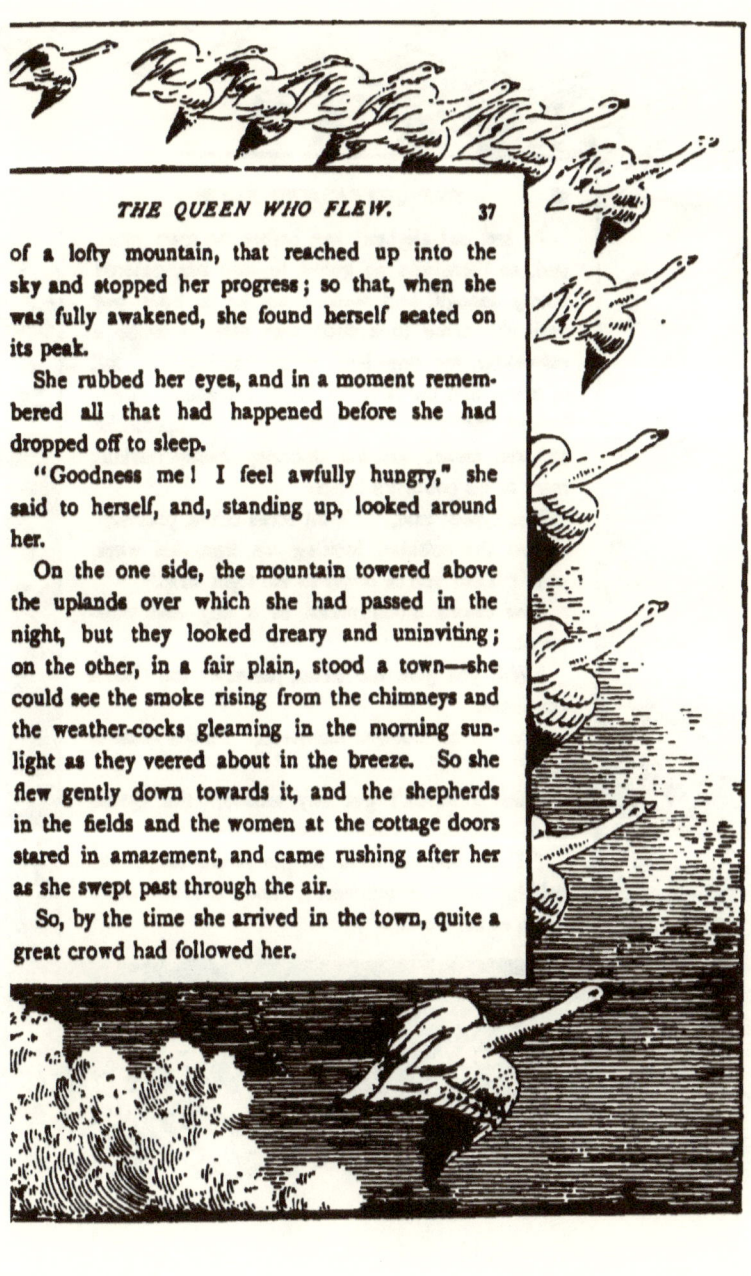

of a lofty mountain, that reached up into the sky and stopped her progress; so that, when she was fully awakened, she found herself seated on its peak.

She rubbed her eyes, and in a moment remembered all that had happened before she had dropped off to sleep.

"Goodness me! I feel awfully hungry," she said to herself, and, standing up, looked around her.

On the one side, the mountain towered above the uplands over which she had passed in the night, but they looked dreary and uninviting; on the other, in a fair plain, stood a town—she could see the smoke rising from the chimneys and the weather-cocks gleaming in the morning sunlight as they veered about in the breeze. So she flew gently down towards it, and the shepherds in the fields and the women at the cottage doors stared in amazement, and came rushing after her as she swept past through the air.

So, by the time she arrived in the town, quite a great crowd had followed her.

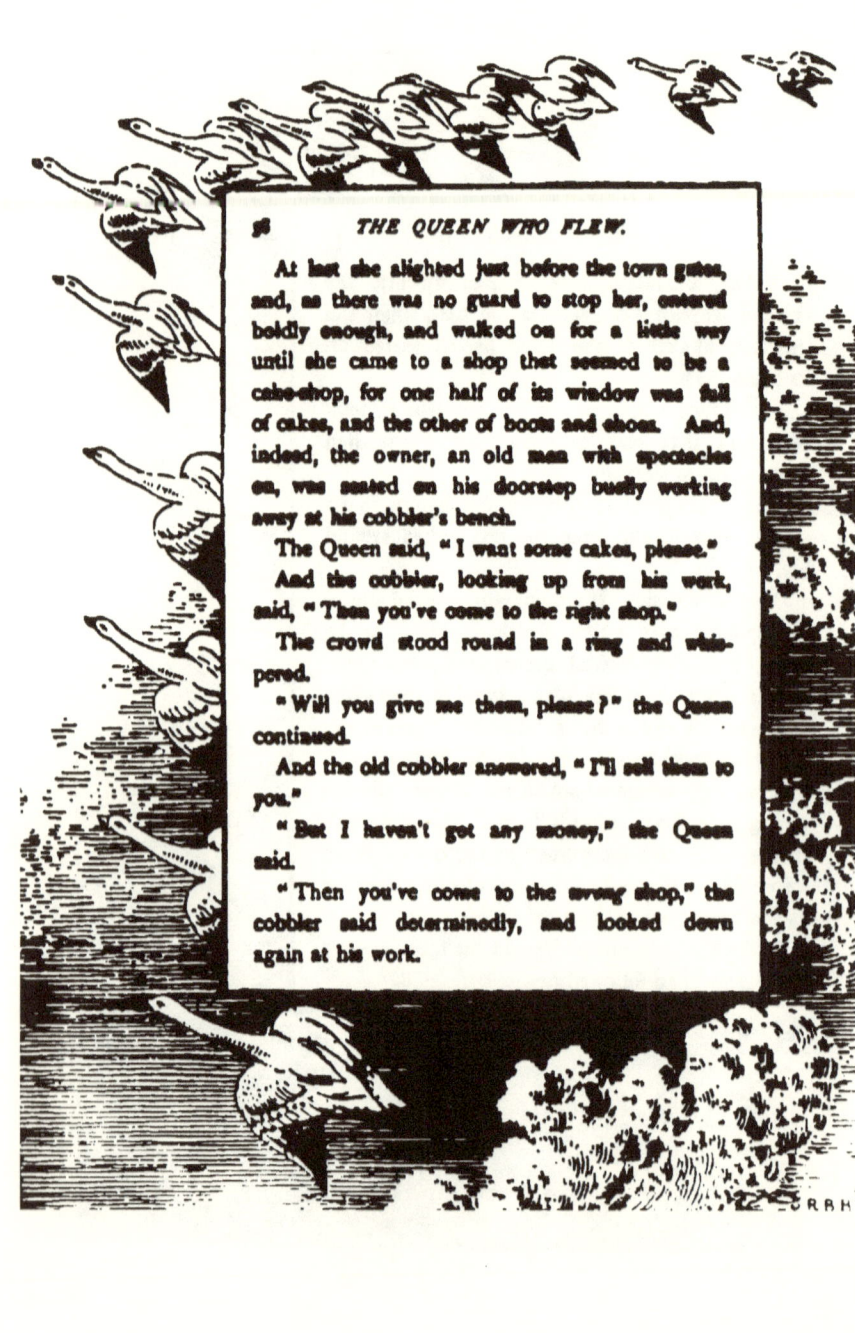

At last she alighted just before the town gates, and, as there was no guard to stop her, entered boldly enough, and walked on for a little way until she came to a shop that seemed to be a cake-shop, for one half of its window was full of cakes, and the other of boots and shoes. And, indeed, the owner, an old man with spectacles on, was seated on his doorstep busily working away at his cobbler's bench.

The Queen said, " I want some cakes, please."

And the cobbler, looking up from his work, said, " Then you've come to the right shop."

The crowd stood round in a ring and whispered.

" Will you give me them, please ? " the Queen continued.

And the old cobbler answered, " I'll sell them to you."

" But I haven't got any money," the Queen said.

" Then you've come to the wrong shop," the cobbler said determinedly, and looked down again at his work.

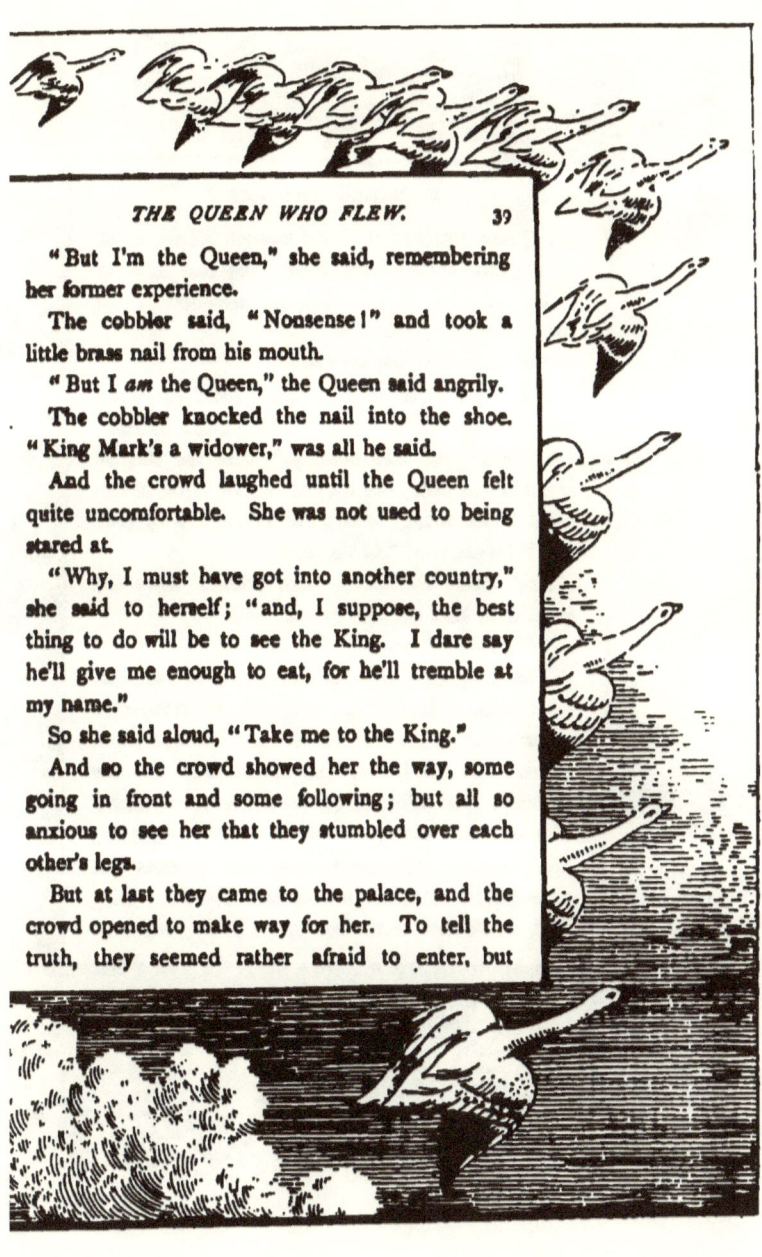

"But I'm the Queen," she said, remembering her former experience.

The cobbler said, "Nonsense!" and took a little brass nail from his mouth.

"But I *am* the Queen," the Queen said angrily.

The cobbler knocked the nail into the shoe. "King Mark's a widower," was all he said.

And the crowd laughed until the Queen felt quite uncomfortable. She was not used to being stared at.

"Why, I must have got into another country," she said to herself; "and, I suppose, the best thing to do will be to see the King. I dare say he'll give me enough to eat, for he'll tremble at my name."

So she said aloud, "Take me to the King."

And so the crowd showed her the way, some going in front and some following; but all so anxious to see her that they stumbled over each other's legs.

But at last they came to the palace, and the crowd opened to make way for her. To tell the truth, they seemed rather afraid to enter, but

the Queen marched in boldly enough till she came
to a great hall. Long before she had time to
make out what it was like, an enormous voice
shouted—

"Who the dickens are you?"

And, looking at the throne, she could make out
an enormous, black-bearded man seated thereon.
He was a great deal more ugly than the Regent
at home had been, and his red eyes twinkled underneath black, shaggy brows, like rubies in a cavern.

"Who are you?" he shouted.

And whilst his fearful voice echoed down the
great dark hall, the Queen answered—

"If you won't tremble, I'll tell you."

The King gave a tremendous roar of laughter.
"Ho, what a joke!" he said, and, to enforce it,
he punched in the ribs the chamberlain who stood
at his right hand, and that so violently that the
wretched man rolled down the throne steps, taking
care to laugh vigorously the whole time, until the
King roared, "Be quiet, you idiot!" when the
chamberlain at once grew silent. Then the King
said, somewhat more softly, "I'll try very hard

not to tremble ; but if I'm very frightened you won't mind, I hope."

And all the courtiers laughed so loud and long at the King's sarcasm, that the Queen had some difficulty in making herself heard.

Then she said, "I am Eldrida, by the grace of God Queen of the Narrowlands and all the Isles."

The King really did seem a little startled.

" What in the world do you want here, then ? " he said, and his red eyes glowed again.

" I want something to eat," the Queen said.

The King seemed lost in thought. "Your Majesty shall have something if——"

" If what ? " the Queen asked.

" If you will marry me," the King said in a tone that was meant to be sweet ; but it rather reminded the Queen of a bull she had once heard grumbling angrily.

She answered decidedly, " I shan't do anything of the sort."

The King said, "Why not ? "

" Because you're a great deal too cruel and ugly,"

the Queen answered. " What did you knock that
poor man down for ? I can't bear that sort of
wickedness. And as for ugliness, why, you're worse
than the Regent himself, and he's the ugliest man
I ever saw."

The King immediately became so convulsed
with rage that he could only roar till the windows
shook out of their frames and shattered on the
ground ; and the Queen stopped her ears with her
fingers, perfectly aghast at the storm she had
raised.

At last the King regained his powers of speech.
" If you don't marry me this very day," he said,
" I'll have you beheaded, I'll have you hanged, I'll
have you thrown from the top of the highest tower
in the town and smash you to pieces."

" You couldn't do anything of the sort," the
Queen said calmly.

Thereupon the King's rage became quite fright-
ful to see, especially for the courtiers who were
nearest him, for he rushed among them and began
to kick them so that they flew into the air ; indeed,
it seemed as if the air was full of them. But, in

the middle of it, he suddenly made a dash at the Queen, and, before she could avoid him, had seized her in his fearful grasp.

"I'll show you if I can't dash you to pieces," he said, and in a minute he had seized her and rushed out into the open air, carrying her like a kitten.

Up to the little door at the foot of the palace tower he went and kicked it open so violently that it banged against the wall and quivered again with the shock, and then round and round and round, and up and up and up, a little dark winding stair, until a sudden burst of light showed that they were at the top.

"Now I'll show you," he muttered, and, shaking her violently he threw her over the side.

But she only dropped softly a short way, and then hovered up again till she played in the air around the tower.

The astonishment of the King was now even greater than his former rage.

"I told you how it would be," the Queen said. "And, if you'll take my advice, you won't lose your

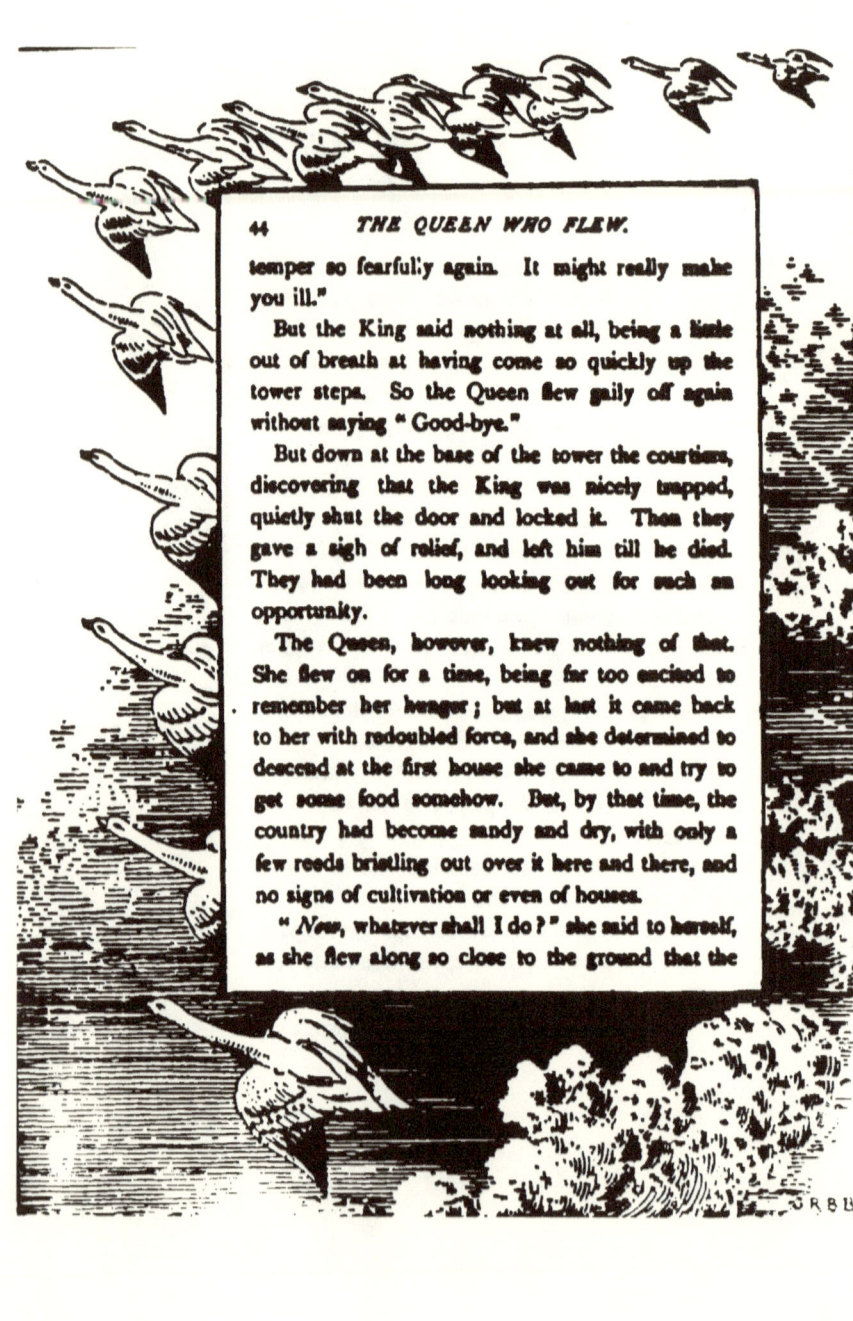

temper so fearfully again. It might really make you ill."

But the King said nothing at all, being a little out of breath at having come so quickly up the tower steps. So the Queen flew gaily off again without saying "Good-bye."

But down at the base of the tower the courtiers, discovering that the King was nicely trapped, quietly shut the door and locked it. Then they gave a sigh of relief, and left him till he died. They had been long looking out for such an opportunity.

The Queen, however, knew nothing of that. She flew on for a time, being far too excited to remember her hunger; but at last it came back to her with redoubled force, and she determined to descend at the first house she came to and try to get some food somehow. But, by that time, the country had become sandy and dry, with only a few reeds bristling out over it here and there, and no signs of cultivation or even of houses.

"*Now*, whatever shall I do?" she said to herself, as she flew along so close to the ground that the

wind of her flight made the sand flit about in little clouds. "I'm so awfully hungry and—— Why, there is some sort of a building !—at least it looks like one."

And there, in a hollow among the sand-dunes, stood a funny little black erection, such as you might see upon a beach.

So the Queen alighted and walked towards the house. In front of the door a cat was sitting—a black cat. But not a magnificent creature with a glossy coat that sits on the rug in front of the drawing-room fire and only drinks cream, deeming mice too vulgar. This was a long-limbed, little creature, that looked half-starved and seemed as if its proper occupation would be stealing along, very lanky and grim in the moonlight, over the dunes to catch rabbits.

So the Queen stopped and looked at the cat, and the cat sat and looked at the Queen.

The black pupils of its yellow eyes dilated and diminished in a most composed manner.

"Poor pussy !" the Queen said, and bent to scratch its neck.

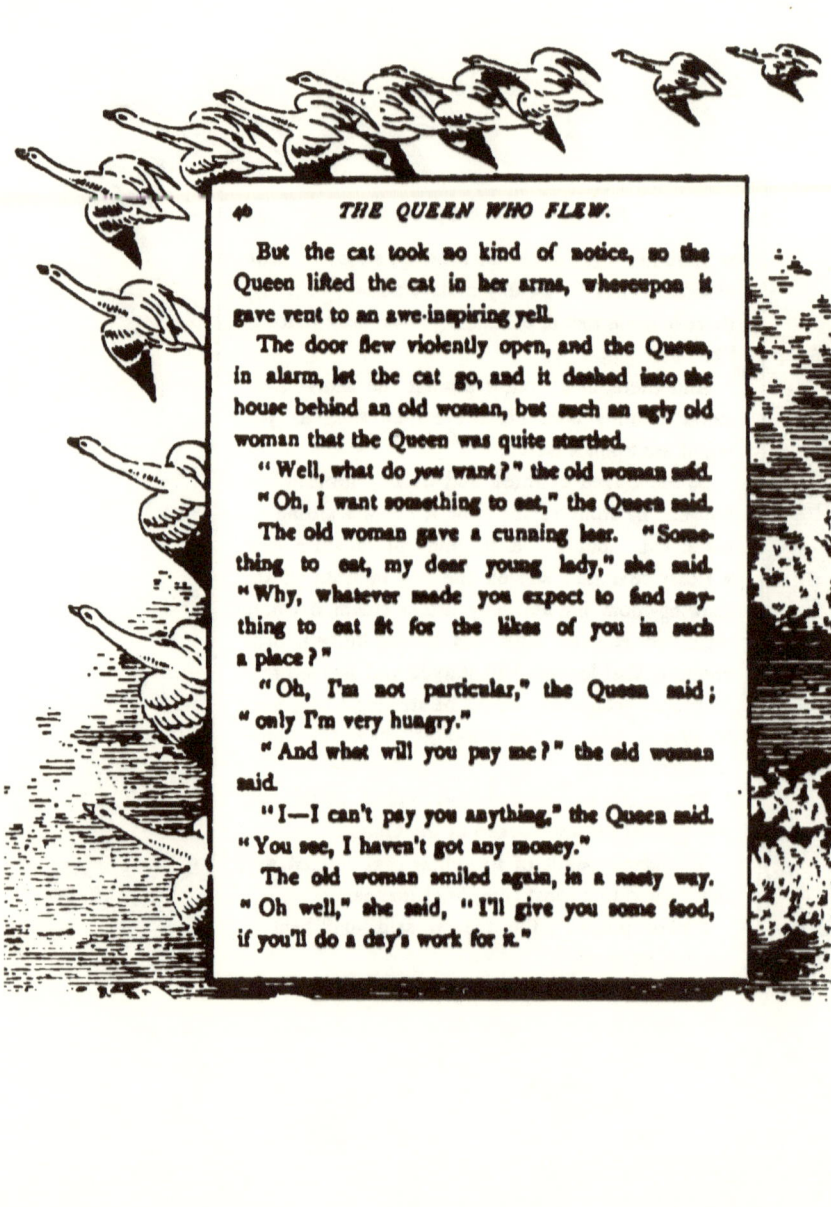

But the cat took no kind of notice, so the Queen lifted the cat in her arms, whereupon it gave vent to an awe-inspiring yell.

The door flew violently open, and the Queen, in alarm, let the cat go, and it dashed into the house behind an old woman, but such an ugly old woman that the Queen was quite startled.

"Well, what do *you* want?" the old woman said.

"Oh, I want something to eat," the Queen said.

The old woman gave a cunning leer. "Something to eat, my dear young lady," she said. "Why, whatever made you expect to find anything to eat fit for the likes of you in such a place?"

"Oh, I'm not particular," the Queen said; "only I'm very hungry."

"And what will you pay me?" the old woman said.

"I—I can't pay you anything," the Queen said. "You see, I haven't got any money."

The old woman smiled again, in a nasty way. "Oh well," she said, "I'll give you some food, if you'll do a day's work for it."

"What sort of work?" the Queen said. "I'm not very clever at work, you know."

"Oh, quite easy work—just goose-herding."

The Queen said, "Oh, I dare say I could do that." .

And the old woman answered, "Oh, very well; come along in, then."

And the Queen followed her into a dirty little room, with only a table and a long bench in it.

But there was a fine wood fire crackling on the hearth, and before it a goose was slowly turning on the spit, so that it did not look quite as dismal as otherwise it might have done.

The Queen sat herself down at the table, and the old woman and the cat were engaged in sitting on the hearth watching the fire.

They did not seem at all talkative, and so the Queen held her peace.

At last the old woman gave a grunt, for the goose was done, and so she got up and found a plate and knife and fork, and put them before the Queen, with the goose on a dish and a large hunk of bread.

"There," she said, "that's all I can give you."

And so, although the food was by no means as dainty as what she would have had at home in the palace, the Queen was so remarkably hungry that she made a much larger meal than she ever remembered to have made.

And all the while the cat sat and stared at her, and seemed to grow positively bigger with staring so much, though when the Queen held out a piece of the goose to it, it merely sniffed contemptuously so that the Queen felt quite humiliated.

"Your cat doesn't seem to be very sociable," she said to the old woman.

And the old woman answered, "Why should he be?" and took up a large twig broom to sweep the hearth with.

That done, she leant upon it and regarded the Queen malevolently.

"Aren't you ever going to finish?" she said.

The Queen answered, "Well, I was rather hungry, you see; but I've finished now. There's no great hurry, is there?"

"I want *my* dinner," the old woman said, with

such an emphasis on the "*my*" that the Queen
was quite amused.

"Why, the goose is there; at least, there's some
of it left."

"But *I* don't like goose," the old woman said.
Her manner was growing more and more peculiar.

"Any one would think you were going to eat
me," the Queen said; and the cat licked its jaws.

"So I am," the old woman said, and her eyes
gleamed.

But the Queen said, "Nonsense!"

"But it's not nonsense," the old woman said;
and the cat began to grow visibly.

"Well, but you didn't say anything about it
before," the Queen said. "I only agreed to herd
your geese."

"But you won't be able to," the old woman
said.

The Queen said, "Why not?"

"Because they're wild ones."

The cat was growing larger and larger, till the
Queen grew positively afraid.

"Well, at any rate, I'll have a try," she said.

E

And the old woman answered, "You may as well save yourself the trouble."

But the Queen insisted, and so they went outside, the old woman carrying her broom, for all the world like a crossing-sweeper.

The great cat rubbed against her skirt and licked its jaws. It was about the size of a lion now.

They came to the back of the house, and there the pen was—a cage covered completely over, and filled with a multitude of geese. The old woman undid the door and threw it wide, and immediately, with a mighty rustle of wings filling the air, the geese swept out of the pen away into the sky.

The old woman chuckled, and the cat crouched itself down as if preparing to spring, lashing its sides with its long tail. But the Queen only smiled, and started off straight into the air, faster even than the geese had gone.

The old woman gave a shriek, and the cat a horrible yell, and then the Queen saw the one mounted upon her broom, and the other without any sort of steed at all, come flying after her.

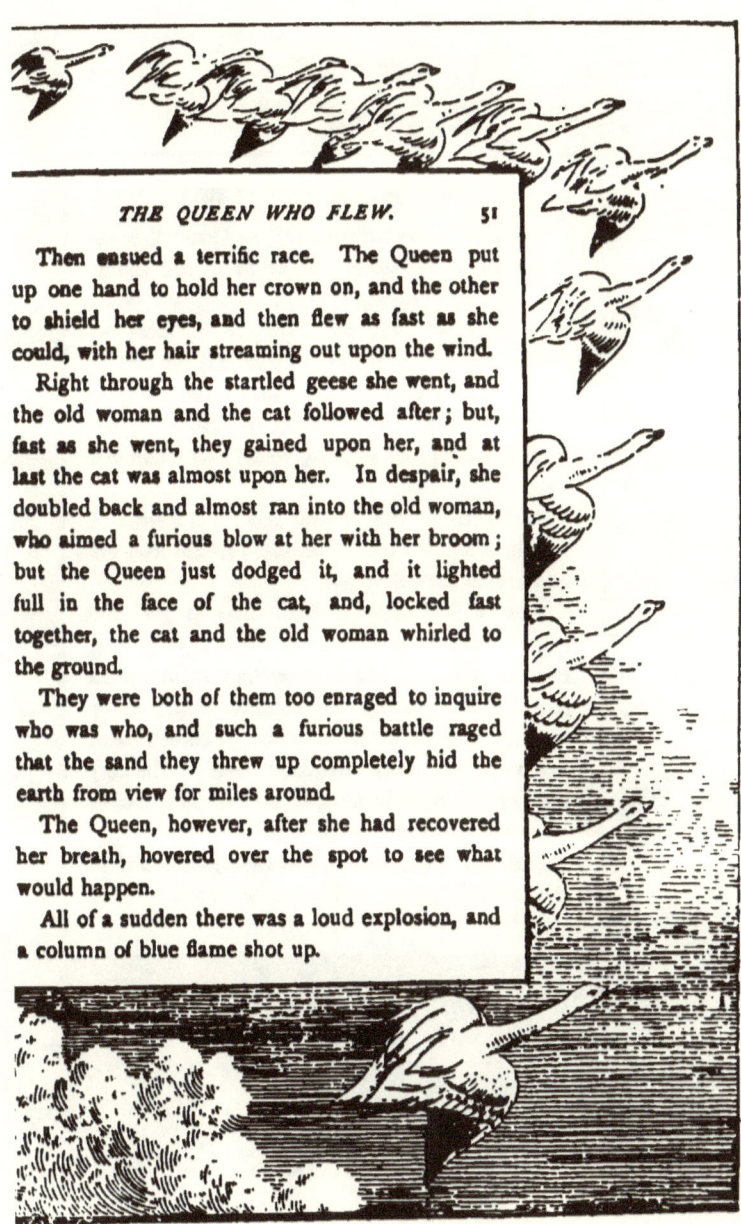

Then ensued a terrific race. The Queen put up one hand to hold her crown on, and the other to shield her eyes, and then flew as fast as she could, with her hair streaming out upon the wind.

Right through the startled geese she went, and the old woman and the cat followed after; but, fast as she went, they gained upon her, and at last the cat was almost upon her. In despair, she doubled back and almost ran into the old woman, who aimed a furious blow at her with her broom; but the Queen just dodged it, and it lighted full in the face of the cat, and, locked fast together, the cat and the old woman whirled to the ground.

They were both of them too enraged to inquire who was who, and such a furious battle raged that the sand they threw up completely hid the earth from view for miles around.

The Queen, however, after she had recovered her breath, hovered over the spot to see what would happen.

All of a sudden there was a loud explosion, and a column of blue flame shot up.

"Now what has happened?" the Queen thought to herself, and prepared to fly off at full speed. But the cloud of sand sailed quietly off down the wind, and, save for a deep hole, there remained no trace of the old woman and her cat.

Just at that moment the Queen heard a mighty rustling of wings, and, looking up, saw the great herd of wild geese swirling round and round her head.

"Dear me!" the Queen said to herself, "I wonder if I could talk to them. Perhaps they will understand bat's language."

Now, it is a rather difficult thing to give you a good idea of what the bat's language is like, because, although one may produce a fairly good imitation by rubbing two corks together, or by blowing through a double button, it doesn't mean any more in bat's language than "Huckery hickyhoo" would in ours, if any one were foolish enough to produce such sounds.

Suffice it, then, to say that the Queen said in the bat's language, "Oh, come, that's a good thing!"

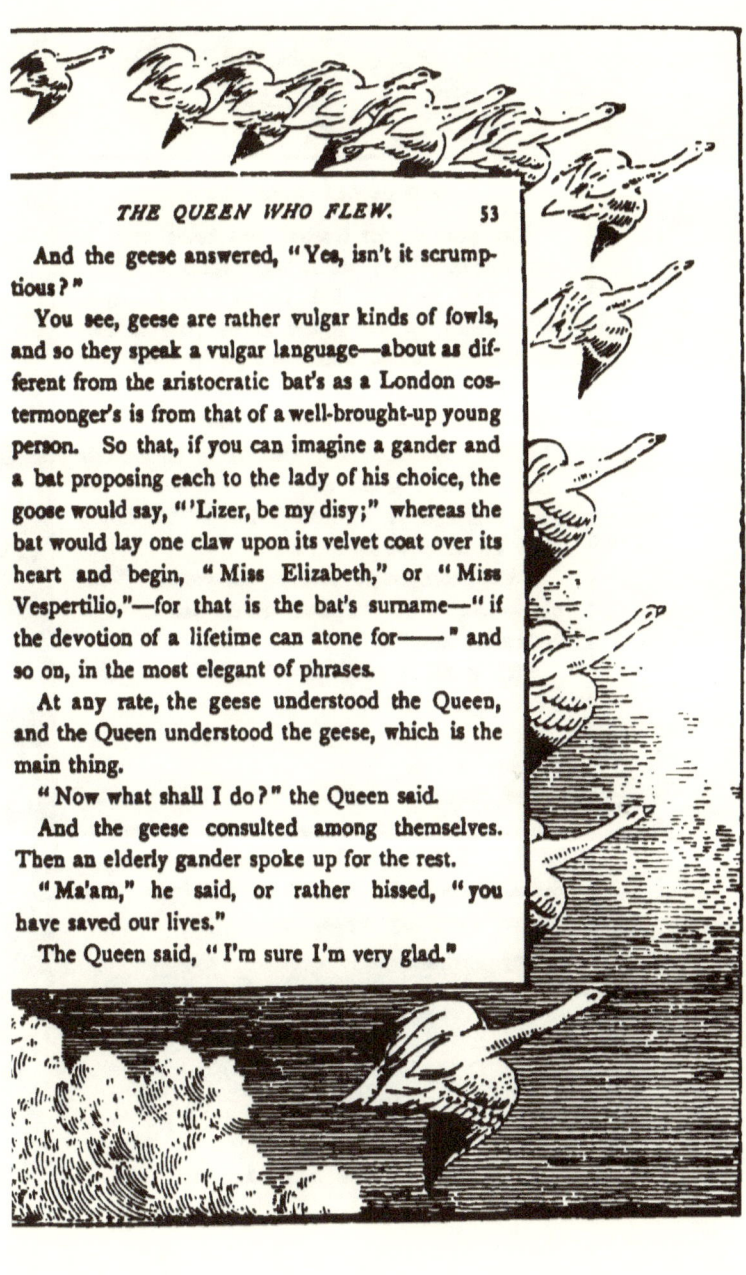

And the geese answered, "Yes, isn't it scrumptious?"

You see, geese are rather vulgar kinds of fowls, and so they speak a vulgar language—about as different from the aristocratic bat's as a London costermonger's is from that of a well-brought-up young person. So that, if you can imagine a gander and a bat proposing each to the lady of his choice, the goose would say, "'Lizer, be my disy;" whereas the bat would lay one claw upon its velvet coat over its heart and begin, "Miss Elizabeth," or "Miss Vespertilio,"—for that is the bat's surname—"if the devotion of a lifetime can atone for——" and so on, in the most elegant of phrases.

At any rate, the geese understood the Queen, and the Queen understood the geese, which is the main thing.

"Now what shall I do?" the Queen said.

And the geese consulted among themselves. Then an elderly gander spoke up for the rest.

"Ma'am," he said, or rather hissed, "you have saved our lives."

The Queen said, "I'm sure I'm very glad."

The poor gander blushed, not being used to speaking in public; but he began again bravely.

"Ma'am, seeing as how you've saved our lives, we've made up our minds to be your faithful servants, and to go where you go, and do what you do."

"I'm sure it's very good of you," the Queen said, not knowing exactly whether to be glad or sorry. "But I don't quite know where I am going; though, as it's getting late in the day, I think I'd better be moving on."

"Why don't you go back to the cottage?" the old gander said. "There'll be no one there to bother you now."

"It's rather a good idea," the Queen said. "I've a good mind to."

"Do," the geese said. "There's a nice river near by."

And, although the latter inducement was inconsiderable, the Queen did as she was asked. In their mad career they had come so great a distance that it was close on nightfall before they reached the cottage again.

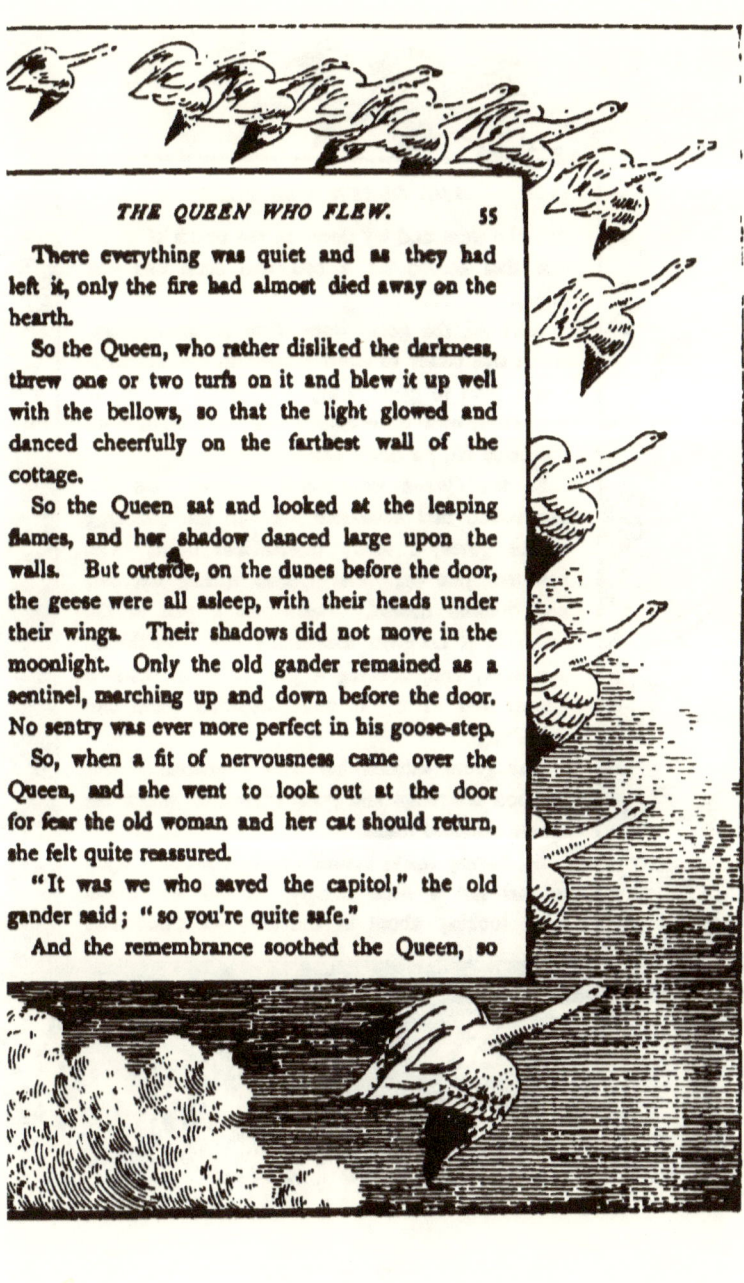

There everything was quiet and as they had left it, only the fire had almost died away on the hearth.

So the Queen, who rather disliked the darkness, threw one or two turfs on it and blew it up well with the bellows, so that the light glowed and danced cheerfully on the farthest wall of the cottage.

So the Queen sat and looked at the leaping flames, and her shadow danced large upon the walls. But outside, on the dunes before the door, the geese were all asleep, with their heads under their wings. Their shadows did not move in the moonlight. Only the old gander remained as a sentinel, marching up and down before the door. No sentry was ever more perfect in his goose-step.

So, when a fit of nervousness came over the Queen, and she went to look out at the door for fear the old woman and her cat should return, she felt quite reassured.

"It was we who saved the capitol," the old gander said; "so you're quite safe."

And the remembrance soothed the Queen, so

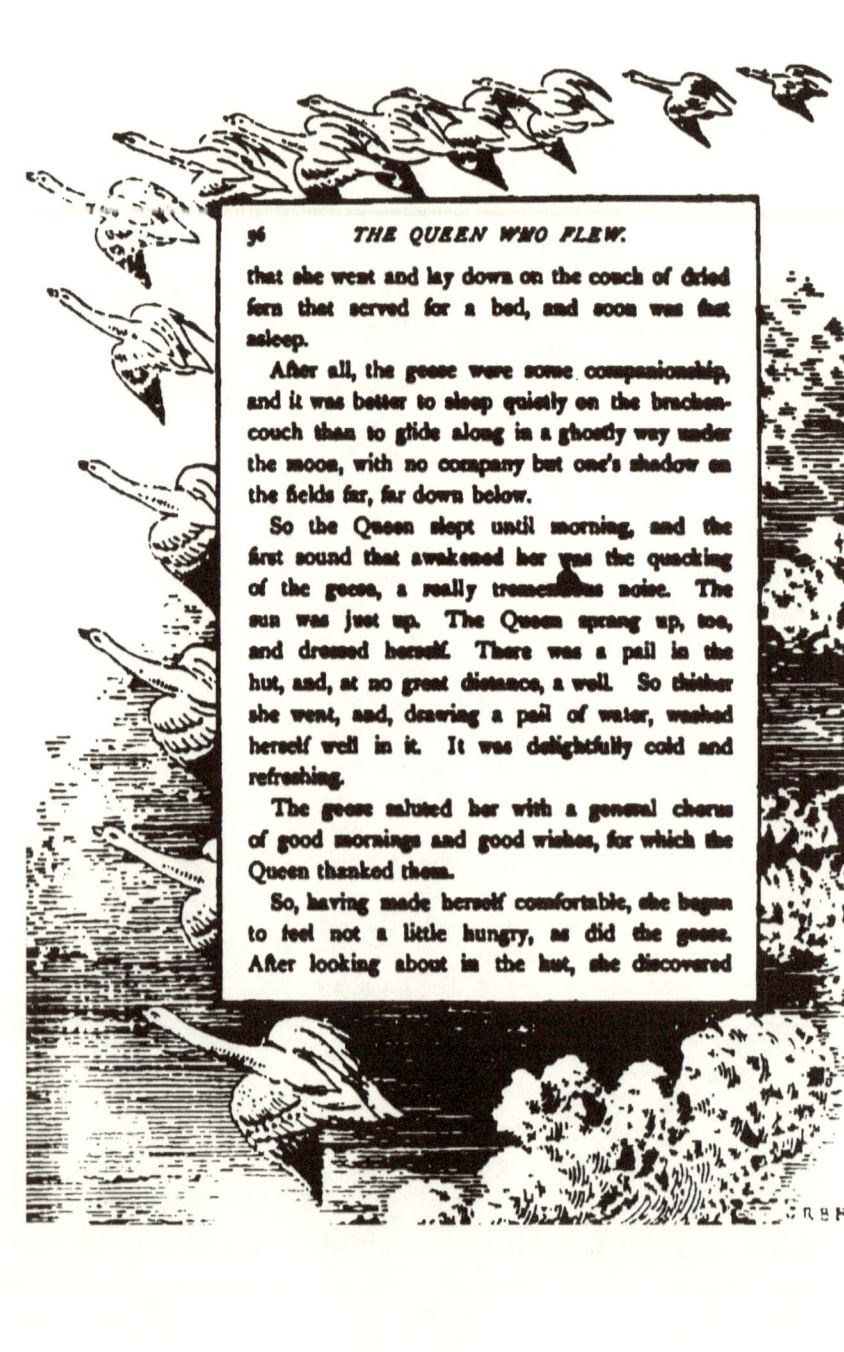

that she went and lay down on the couch of dried fern that served for a bed, and soon was fast asleep.

After all, the geese were some companionship, and it was better to sleep quietly on the bracken-couch than to glide along in a ghostly way under the moon, with no company but one's shadow on the fields far, far down below.

So the Queen slept until morning, and the first sound that awakened her was the quacking of the geese, a really tremendous noise. The sun was just up. The Queen sprang up, too, and dressed herself. There was a pail in the hut, and, at no great distance, a well. So thither she went, and, drawing a pail of water, washed herself well in it. It was delightfully cold and refreshing.

The geese saluted her with a general chorus of good mornings and good wishes, for which the Queen thanked them.

So, having made herself comfortable, she began to feel not a little hungry, as did the geese. After looking about in the hut, she discovered

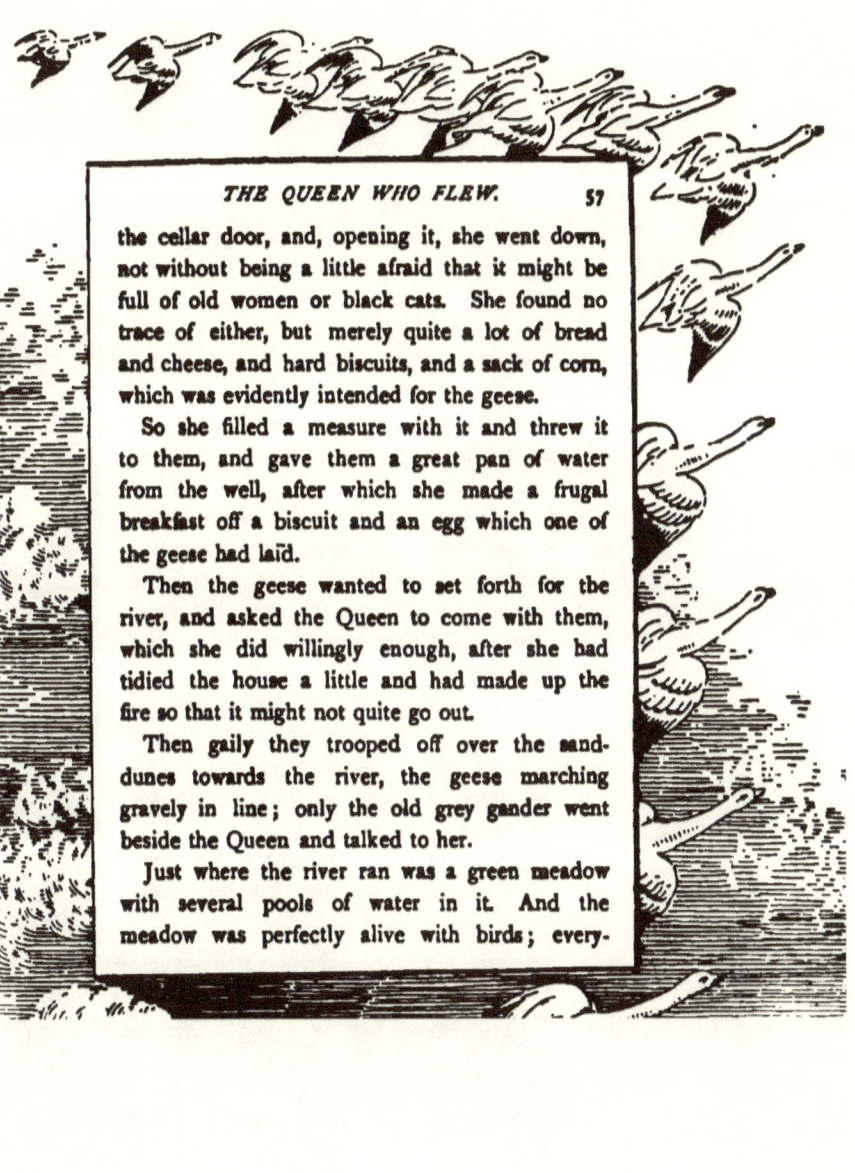

the cellar door, and, opening it, she went down, not without being a little afraid that it might be full of old women or black cats. She found no trace of either, but merely quite a lot of bread and cheese, and hard biscuits, and a sack of corn, which was evidently intended for the geese.

So she filled a measure with it and threw it to them, and gave them a great pan of water from the well, after which she made a frugal breakfast off a biscuit and an egg which one of the geese had laïd.

Then the geese wanted to set forth for the river, and asked the Queen to come with them, which she did willingly enough, after she had tidied the house a little and had made up the fire so that it might not quite go out.

Then gaily they trooped off over the sand-dunes towards the river, the geese marching gravely in line; only the old grey gander went beside the Queen and talked to her.

Just where the river ran was a green meadow with several pools of water in it. And the meadow was perfectly alive with birds; every-

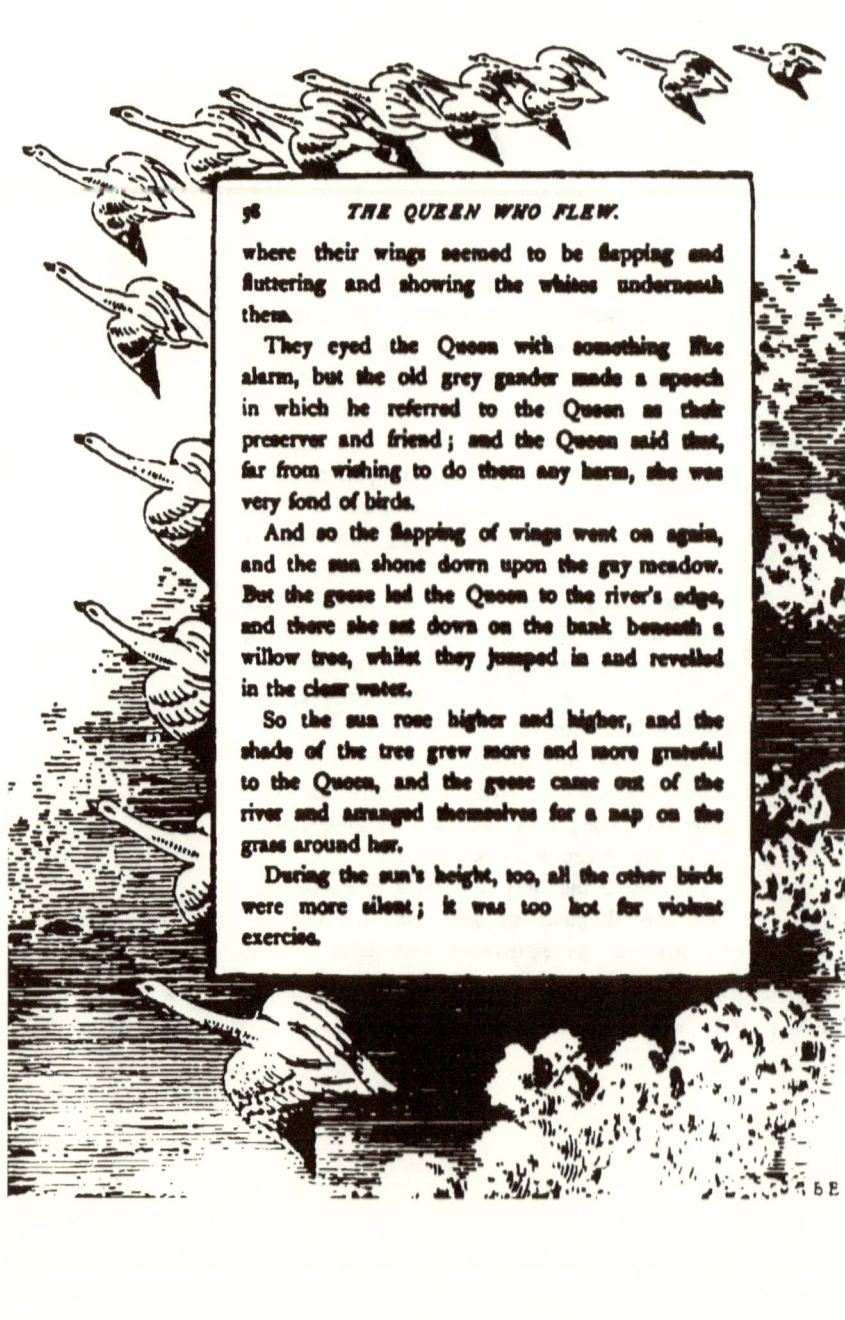

where their wings seemed to be flapping and
fluttering and showing the whites underneath
them.

They eyed the Queen with something like
alarm, but the old grey gander made a speech
in which he referred to the Queen as their
preserver and friend; and the Queen said that,
far from wishing to do them any harm, she was
very fond of birds.

And so the flapping of wings went on again,
and the sun shone down upon the gay meadow.
But the geese led the Queen to the river's edge,
and there she sat down on the bank beneath a
willow tree, whilst they jumped in and revelled
in the clear water.

So the sun rose higher and higher, and the
shade of the tree grew more and more grateful
to the Queen, and the geese came out of the
river and arranged themselves for a nap on the
grass around her.

During the sun's height, too, all the other birds
were more silent; it was too hot for violent
exercise.

So the river gurgled among the rushes, and they rustled and bent their heads, and the willow leaves forgot to tremble for want of a breeze. And the great, placid flow of the river was without a dimple on its face, save when a fish sprang gleaming out after a low-flying midge.

So the Queen felt happy and contented, and she, too, dozed off into a little nap, whilst the woolly clouds slowly sailed across the blue heaven.

But towards evening the birds all woke up; the peewits flew off in a flock to the marshy flats down the river, and the snipe whirred away to the mud-banks, and the geese arose and cropped the greensward with their bills.

And then, towards sunset, they all rose in the air, and the Queen with them, and went whirling round in great clouds of rustling pinions, dyed red in the sunset, geese and peewits, and snipe and herons, all wheeling about in sheer delight of life; until, when the sun was almost down, the geese, with a great cry of farewell, flew off through the gloaming with the Queen towards the hut.

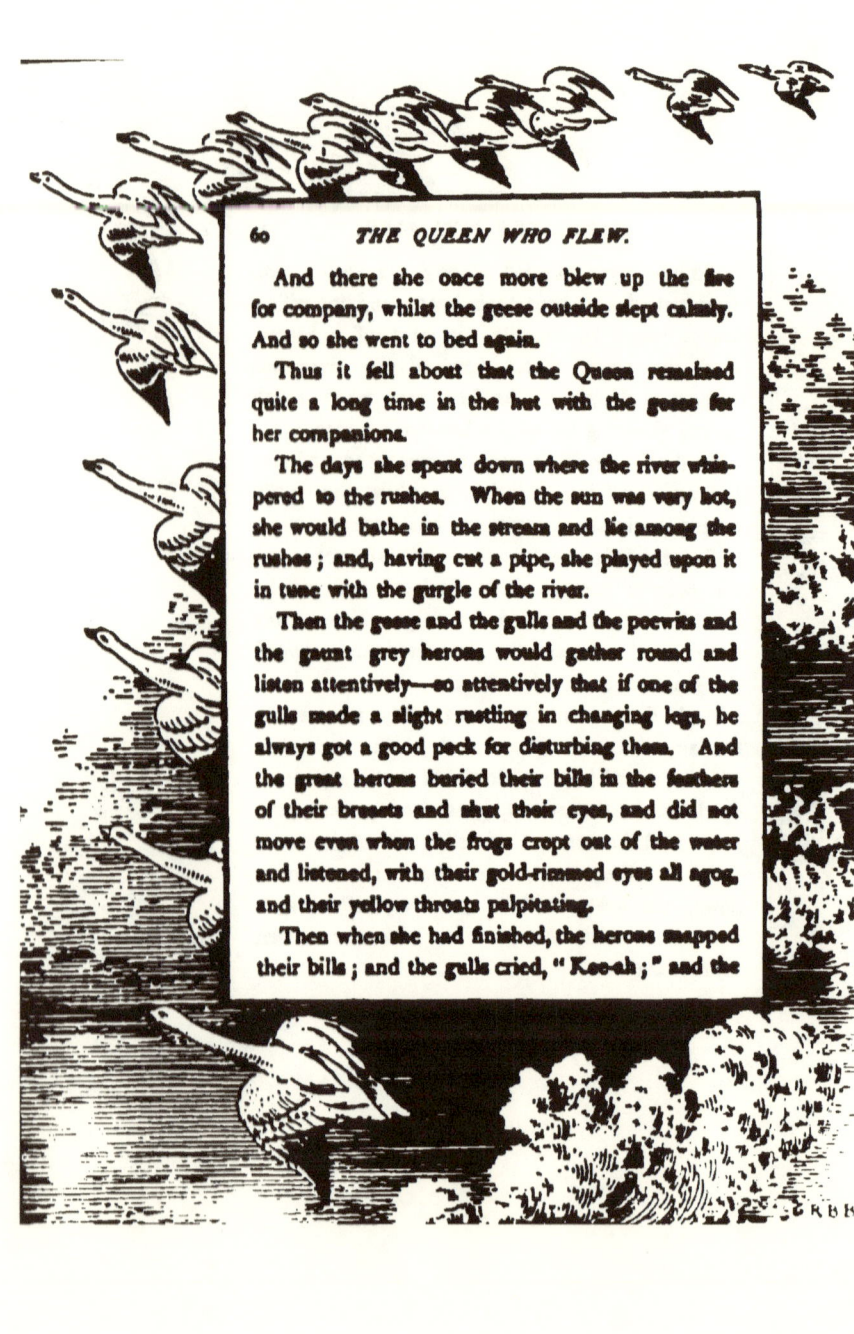

And there she once more blew up the fire for company, whilst the geese outside slept calmly. And so she went to bed again.

Thus it fell about that the Queen remained quite a long time in the hut with the geese for her companions.

The days she spent down where the river whispered to the rushes. When the sun was very hot, she would bathe in the stream and lie among the rushes ; and, having cut a pipe, she played upon it in tune with the gurgle of the river.

Then the geese and the gulls and the peewits and the gaunt grey herons would gather round and listen attentively—so attentively that if one of the gulls made a slight rustling in changing legs, he always got a good peck for disturbing them. And the great herons buried their bills in the feathers of their breasts and shut their eyes, and did not move even when the frogs crept out of the water and listened, with their gold-rimmed eyes all agog, and their yellow throats palpitating.

Then when she had finished, the herons snapped their bills ; and the gulls cried, " Kee-ah ; " and the

peewits, "Peewit;" and the geese hissed, with their necks stretched out—but that too signified applause.

As for the frogs, they made haste to spring with a plop into the rushes, without any applause at all; but that was because the herons had opened their eyes and were stalking towards them.

So the Queen was very much beloved in the bird-meadow, and the gulls would come out of the shining pools to greet her when she came in the freshness of the morning, and the herons would lay fish at her feet, and the peewits would perch upon her shoulder and fly round her head, and the whirr of wings was everywhere. But the geese were her guard of honour.

One morning before they set out for the bird-meadow, whilst the Queen was engaged in tidying up the hut, the geese suddenly set up a most terrible hissing and quacking.

"Dear me!" the Queen said, "there'll be a terrible rain-storm soon."

But at that moment the old grey gander came running excitedly into the hut.

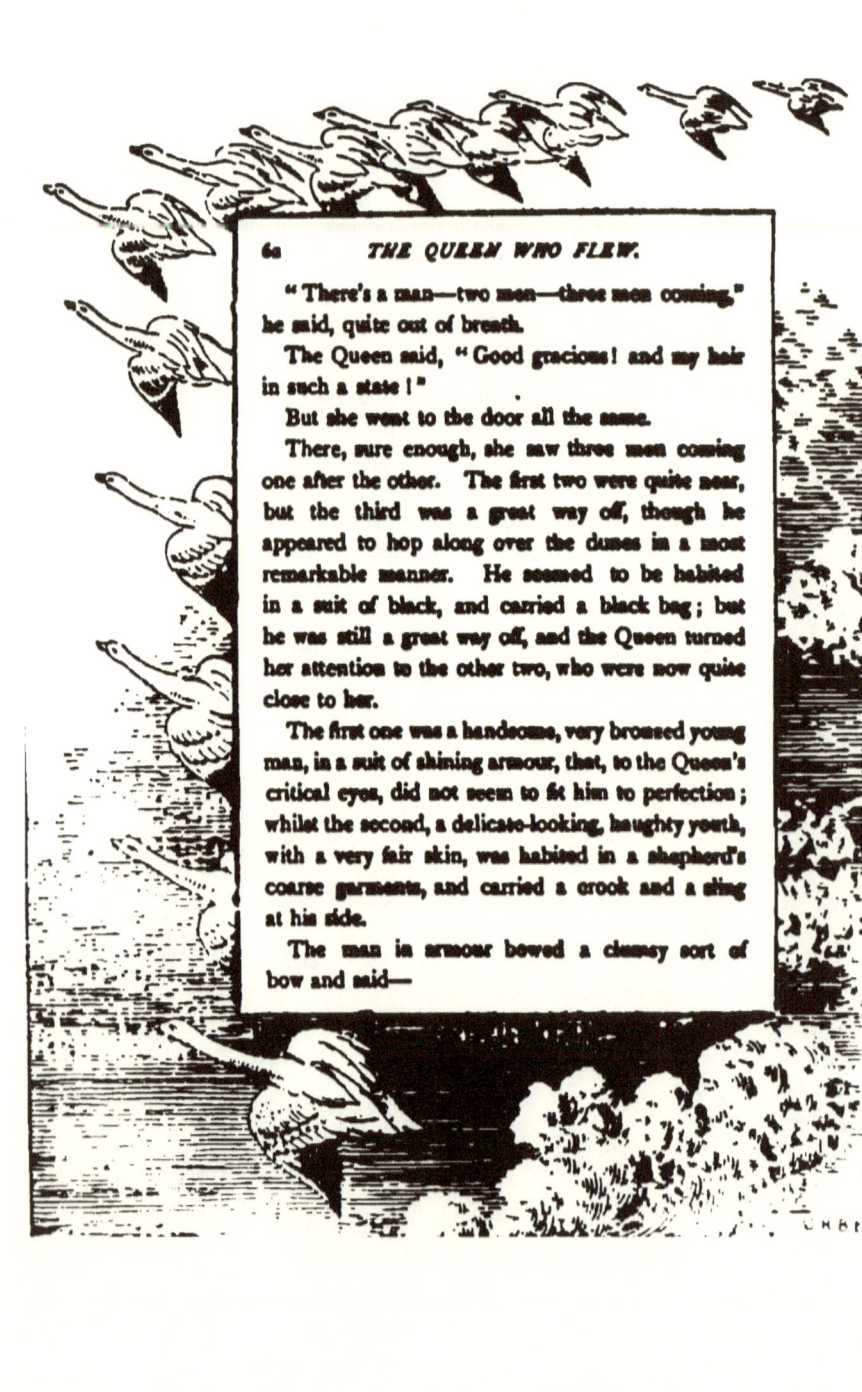

" There's a man—two men—three men coming,"
he said, quite out of breath.

The Queen said, " Good gracious! and my hair
in such a state ! "

But she went to the door all the same.

There, sure enough, she saw three men coming
one after the other.   The first two were quite near,
but the third was a great way off, though he
appeared to hop along over the dunes in a most
remarkable manner.   He seemed to be habited
in a suit of black, and carried a black bag ; but
he was still a great way off, and the Queen turned
her attention to the other two, who were now quite
close to her.

The first one was a handsome, very bronzed young
man, in a suit of shining armour, that, to the Queen's
critical eyes, did not seem to fit him to perfection ;
whilst the second, a delicate-looking, haughty youth,
with a very fair skin, was habited in a shepherd's
coarse garments, and carried a crook and a sling
at his side.

The man in armour bowed a clumsy sort of
bow and said—

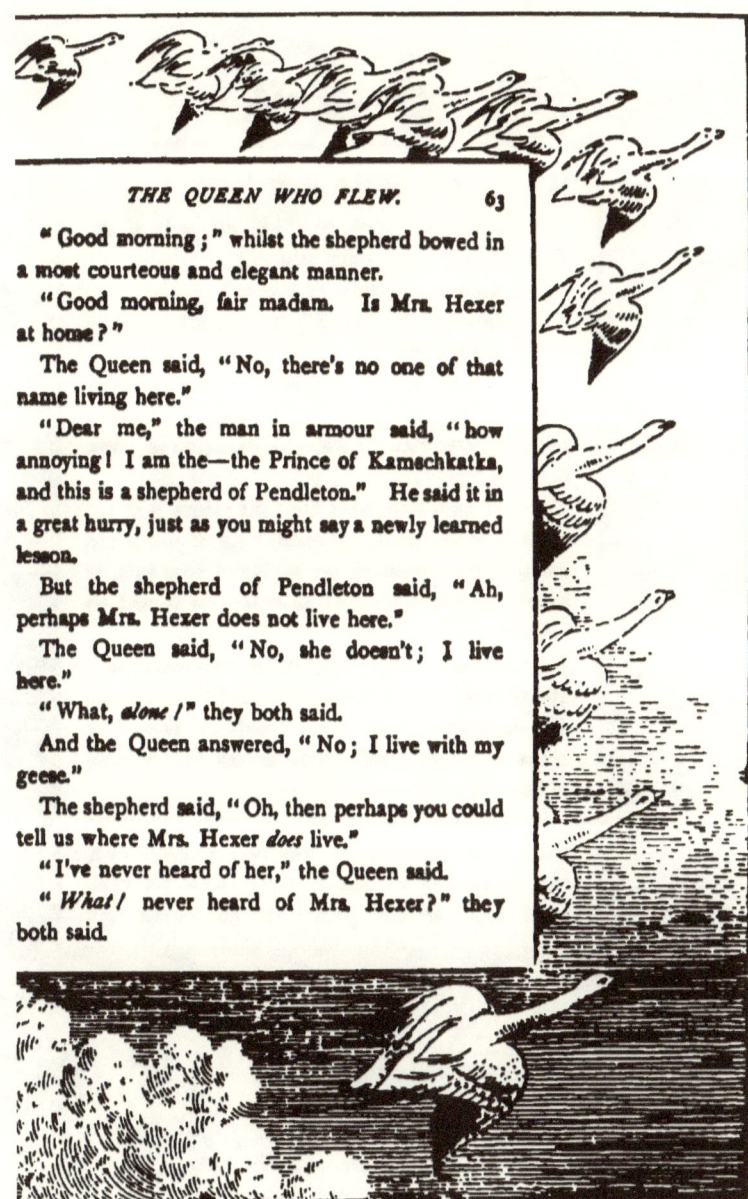

" Good morning ; " whilst the shepherd bowed in a most courteous and elegant manner.

" Good morning, fair madam. Is Mrs. Hexer at home ? "

The Queen said, " No, there's no one of that name living here."

" Dear me," the man in armour said, " how annoying! I am the—the Prince of Kamschkatka, and this is a shepherd of Pendleton." He said it in a great hurry, just as you might say a newly learned lesson.

But the shepherd of Pendleton said, " Ah, perhaps Mrs. Hexer does not live here."

The Queen said, " No, she doesn't ; I live here."

" What, *alone* /" they both said.

And the Queen answered, " No ; I live with my geese."

The shepherd said, " Oh, then perhaps you could tell us where Mrs. Hexer *does* live."

" I've never heard of her," the Queen said.

" *What* / never heard of Mrs. Hexer ? " they both said.

"The famous witch who has the well of the Elixir of Life," the prince said.

But the shepherd said, "Of love."

The mention of "witch" brought something to the Queen's mind.

"There used to be a horrible old woman who lived here with a great black cat," she said. "Perhaps *she* was Mrs. Hexer; but she disappeared some time ago."

"That must have been her," the prince said.

And the shepherd continued, "Ah, if you would let us sit for a while on the coping of your well, or even give us a draught of its water, we should be infinitely obliged to you."

The Queen said, "Oh, you're very welcome," and turned into the house to get her bucket, when she was astonished to see a coal-black thing with horns and a long tail sitting in the very middle of her fire.

She rubbed her eyes in surprise, and when she looked again there was only a gentleman, clad in an elegant suit of black, with his coal-black hair carefully parted in the middle and

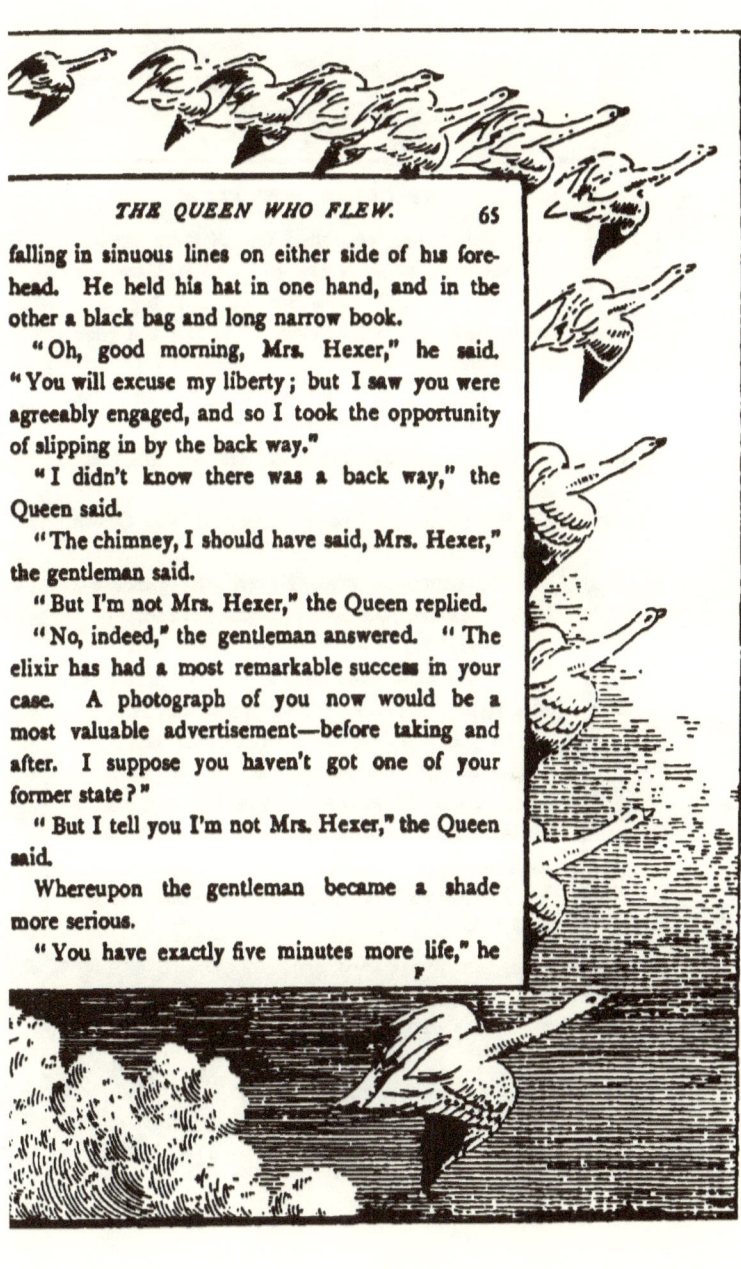

falling in sinuous lines on either side of his fore-
head. He held his hat in one hand, and in the
other a black bag and long narrow book.

"Oh, good morning, Mrs. Hexer," he said.
"You will excuse my liberty; but I saw you were
agreeably engaged, and so I took the opportunity
of slipping in by the back way."

"I didn't know there was a back way," the
Queen said.

"The chimney, I should have said, Mrs. Hexer,"
the gentleman said.

"But I'm not Mrs. Hexer," the Queen replied.

"No, indeed," the gentleman answered. "The
elixir has had a most remarkable success in your
case. A photograph of you now would be a
most valuable advertisement—before taking and
after. I suppose you haven't got one of your
former state?"

"But I tell you I'm not Mrs. Hexer," the Queen
said.

Whereupon the gentleman became a shade
more serious.

"You have exactly five minutes more life," he

F

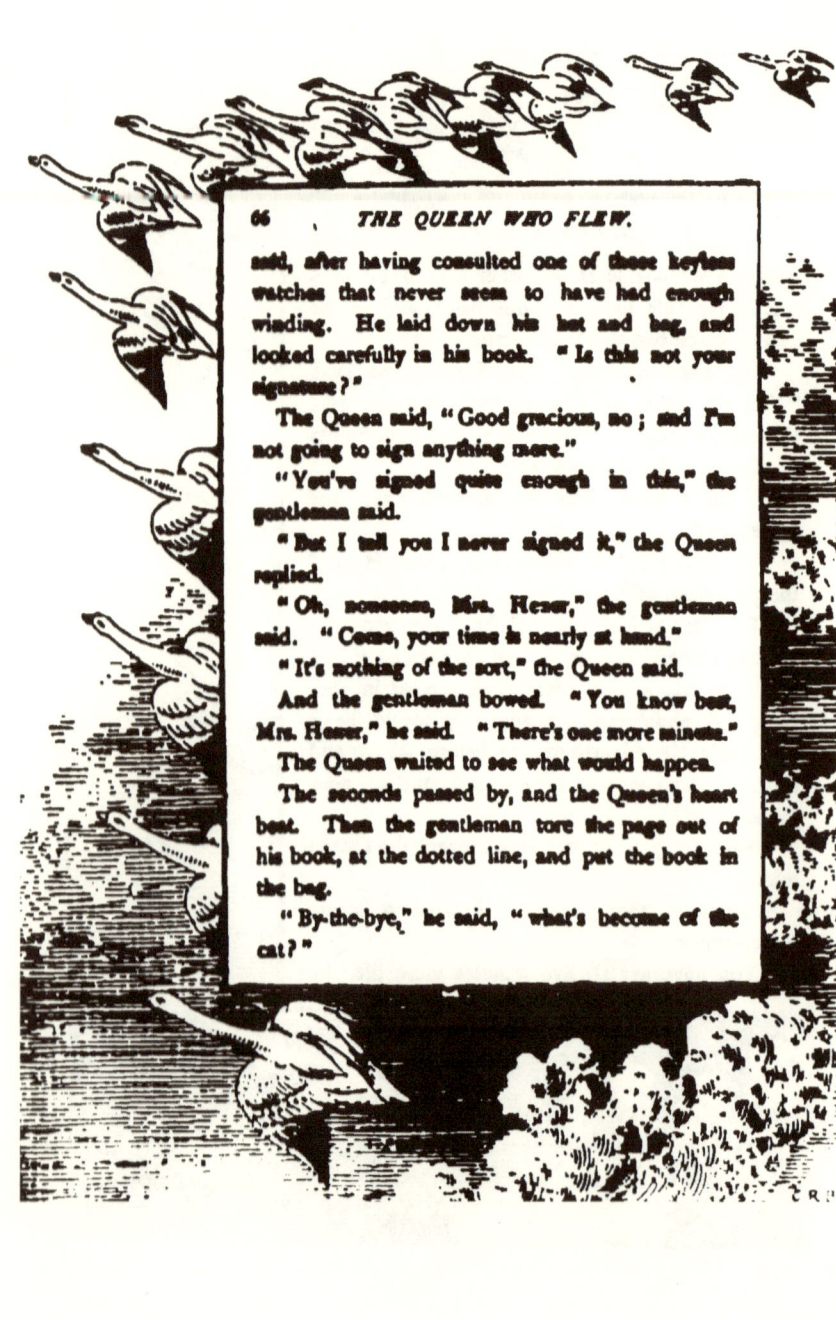

said, after having consulted one of those keyless watches that never seem to have had enough winding. He laid down his hat and bag, and looked carefully in his book. " Is this not your signature ? "

The Queen said, " Good gracious, no ; and I'm not going to sign anything more."

" You've signed quite enough in this," the gentleman said.

" But I tell you I never signed it," the Queen replied.

" Oh, nonsense, Mrs. Hexer," the gentleman said. " Come, your time is nearly at hand."

" It's nothing of the sort," the Queen said.

And the gentleman bowed. " You know best, Mrs. Hexer," he said. " There's one more minute."

The Queen waited to see what would happen.

The seconds passed by, and the Queen's heart beat. Then the gentleman tore the page out of his book, at the dotted line, and put the book in the bag.

" By-the-bye," he said, " what's become of the cat ? "

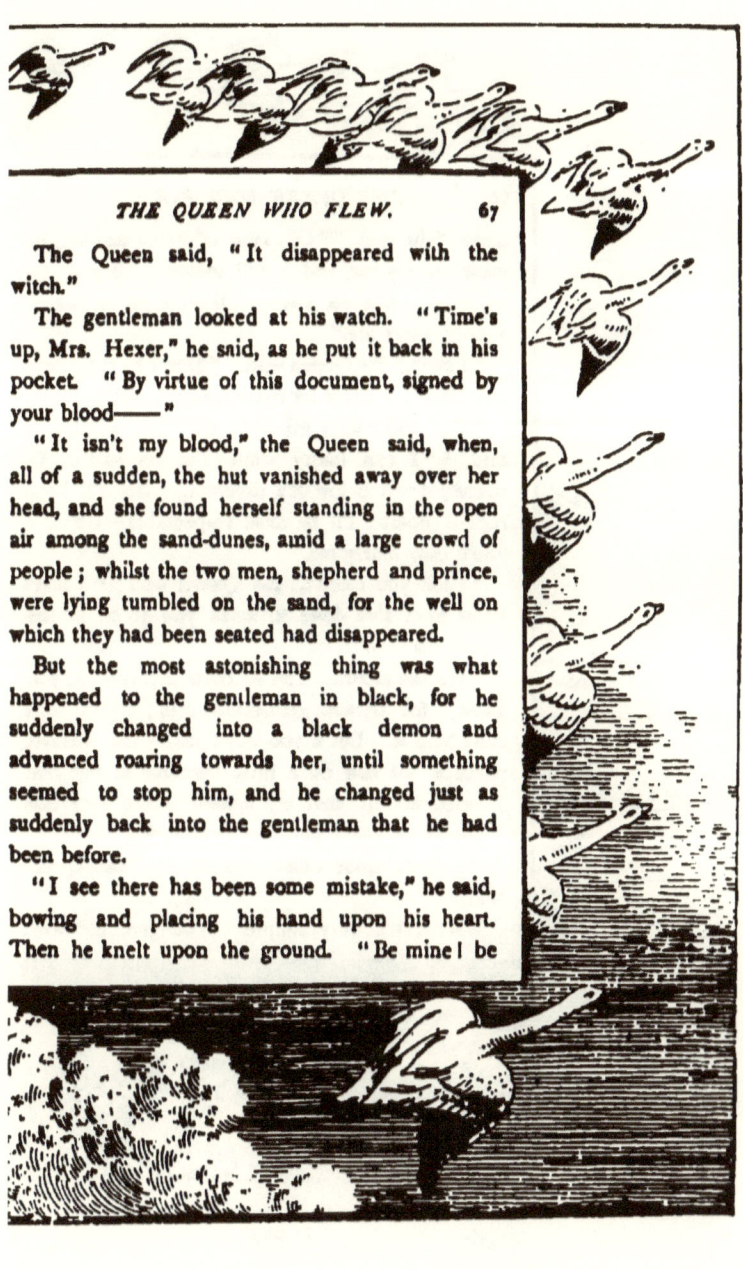

The Queen said, "It disappeared with the witch."

The gentleman looked at his watch. "Time's up, Mrs. Hexer," he said, as he put it back in his pocket. "By virtue of this document, signed by your blood——"

"It isn't my blood," the Queen said, when, all of a sudden, the hut vanished away over her head, and she found herself standing in the open air among the sand-dunes, amid a large crowd of people; whilst the two men, shepherd and prince, were lying tumbled on the sand, for the well on which they had been seated had disappeared.

But the most astonishing thing was what happened to the gentleman in black, for he suddenly changed into a black demon and advanced roaring towards her, until something seemed to stop him, and he changed just as suddenly back into the gentleman that he had been before.

"I see there has been some mistake," he said, bowing and placing his hand upon his heart. Then he knelt upon the ground. "Be mine! be

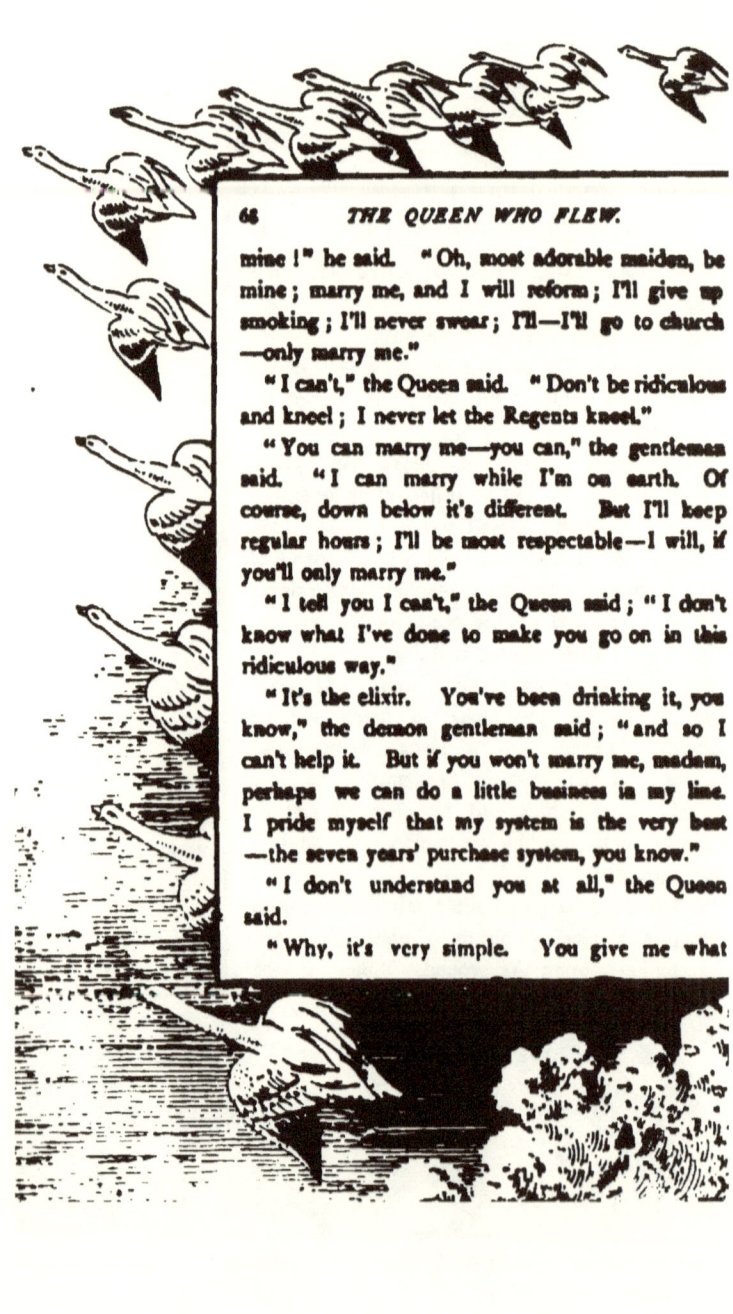

mine !" he said.   "Oh, most adorable maiden, be
mine ; marry me, and I will reform; I'll give up
smoking ; I'll never swear; I'll—I'll go to church
—only marry me."

"I can't," the Queen said.   "Don't be ridiculous
and kneel ; I never let the Regents kneel."

"You can marry me—you can," the gentleman
said.   "I can marry while I'm on earth.   Of
course, down below it's different.   But I'll keep
regular hours ; I'll be most respectable—I will, if
you'll only marry me."

"I tell you I can't," the Queen said; "I don't
know what I've done to make you go on in this
ridiculous way."

"It's the elixir.   You've been drinking it, you
know," the demon gentleman said; "and so I
can't help it.   But if you won't marry me, madam,
perhaps we can do a little business in my line.
I pride myself that my system is the very best
—the seven years' purchase system, you know."

"I don't understand you at all," the Queen
said.

"Why, it's very simple.   You give me what

I want, and I will re-erect for you the desirable family residence that stood here, with all its advantages—the delightfully secluded spot, the landscape, the well of pure water, and the fowl-house with its stock of geese. Come, let me fill you up a form."

"Yes, but what do I have to do for it?" the Queen said.

And he answered, "Oh, a mere trifle—only a formality."

"But what *is* it?"

"Oh, you only give me your soul—it's nothing at all."

"*My soul!*" the Queen said. "Certainly not."

"But I'll make you rich," the gentleman said.

"I'm quite rich enough already," the Queen answered.

"I'll make you powerful—make you a great queen."

"I'm one already, thanks," the Queen said.

"I'll give you a broom that you can fly on," the gentleman remarked.

"I can fly without a broom," the Queen said.

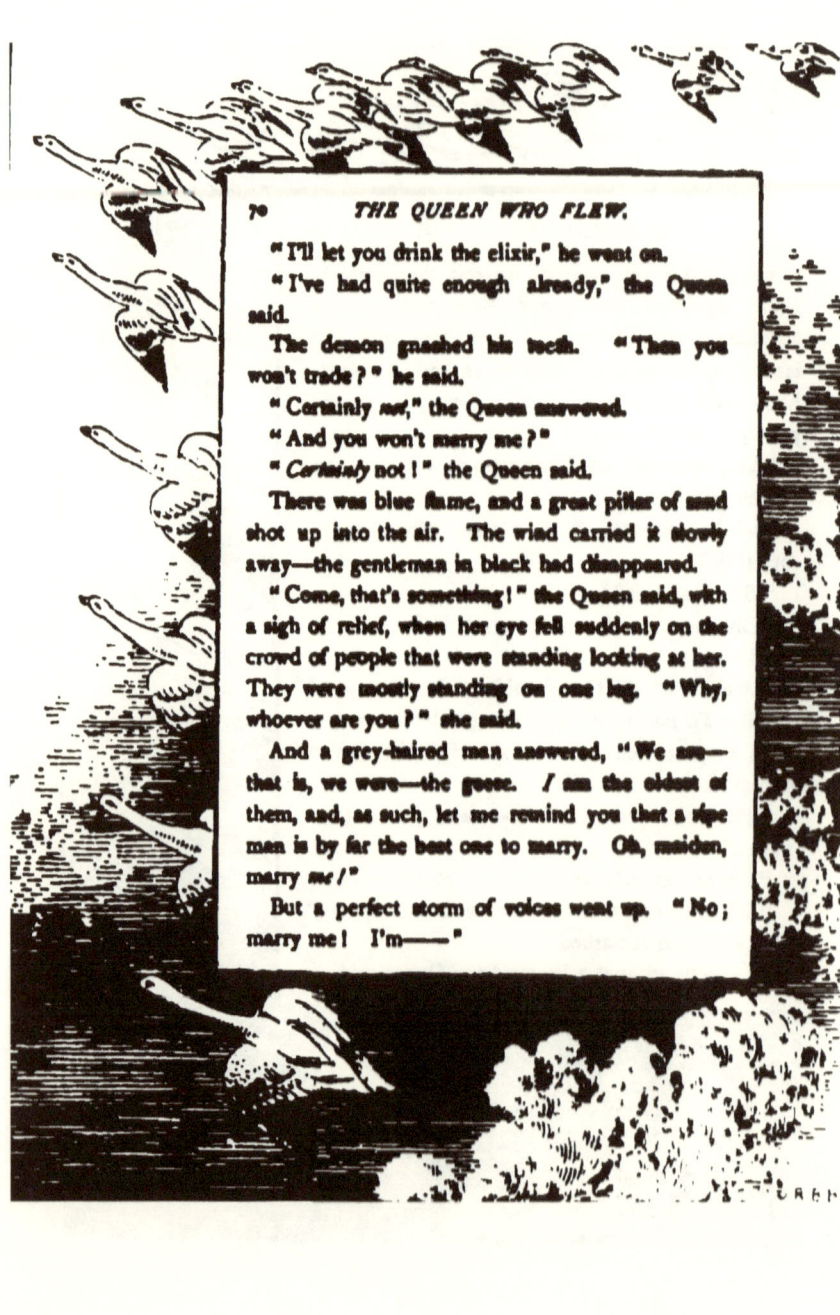

"I'll let you drink the elixir," he went on.

"I've had quite enough already," the Queen said.

The demon gnashed his teeth. "Then you won't trade?" he said.

"Certainly *not*," the Queen answered.

"And you won't marry me?"

"*Certainly* not!" the Queen said.

There was blue flame, and a great pillar of sand shot up into the air. The wind carried it slowly away—the gentleman in black had disappeared.

"Come, that's something!" the Queen said, with a sigh of relief, when her eye fell suddenly on the crowd of people that were standing looking at her. They were mostly standing on one leg. "Why, whoever are you?" she said.

And a grey-haired man answered, "We are— that is, we were—the geese. *I* am the oldest of them, and, as such, let me remind you that a ripe man is by far the best one to marry. Oh, maiden, marry *me*!"

But a perfect storm of voices went up. "No; marry me! I'm——"

But the Queen held up her hand to command silence.

"Don't make such a fearful noise. I can't even hear myself think. I'm not going to marry any of you, though you were very nice, dear geese, and I was very fond of you."

"No; the lady is going to marry me!" a voice said, and the man in shepherd's clothes stept forth.

"No, marry me!" the man in armour said.

"I'm a prince. I will make you a princess," the man in shepherd's clothes said.

"I'm a shepherd," the man dressed like a prince said. "A shepherd is a far better match for a goose-girl than a prince is."

"But why were either of you so deceitful?" the Queen said. "Because it's so ridiculous. You don't look like a shepherd, prince—your skin is much too fair; and you are much too brawny to be a prince, shepherd."

"Well, I thought it was not quite respectable for a prince to be seen visiting a witch, and so I changed clothes with the shepherd here."

"And I changed clothes with the prince because I had seen you from afar, and had loved you; and because I thought a prince would have seemed more splendid than a common shepherd."

"But you were both wrong to try to deceive me," the Queen said. "As for you, prince, I will not marry you to be made a princess, for I am a Queen already; and for you, shepherd, I will not marry you to become a shepherdess, for I am goose-girl already, though my flock has turned back from its goose-shape again. But how did you become geese, anyhow?" she asked of them.

And he who had been the old grey gander answered, "The witch turned us into it when we came to ask for the Elixir of Love."

"Dear me!" the Queen said. "Does love make such geese of people?"

And the shepherd in prince's clothing said, "I'm afraid it does."

"You see, it was as I said," the old grey gander said; "those young men are all fools. You had much better marry me."

He had no sooner said the words than a perfect whirlwind of shouts arose.

"Marry me!" "No, marry me!" "Me!" "Me!" "Me!"

The Queen put her fingers to her ears. "If you don't be quiet I'll fly away altogether," she said.

But it produced no effect at all; the sound of voices went on just like the sound of surf on a pebbly shore.

"Oh, I can't stand it," the Queen said. "And to think that it is to go on like this for ever and ever, and all because of this horrible elixir! I shall fly right away from it."

And she quietly rose and sailed away in the air, and the last she saw of the geese was that they were feebly trying to fly after her, waving their arms frantically as if they had been wings.

The Queen flew straight up into the air, and she had reached a dizzy height before she thought of what she was doing.

To tell the truth, she was a little sorrowful at the thought of leaving the geese; for, with the

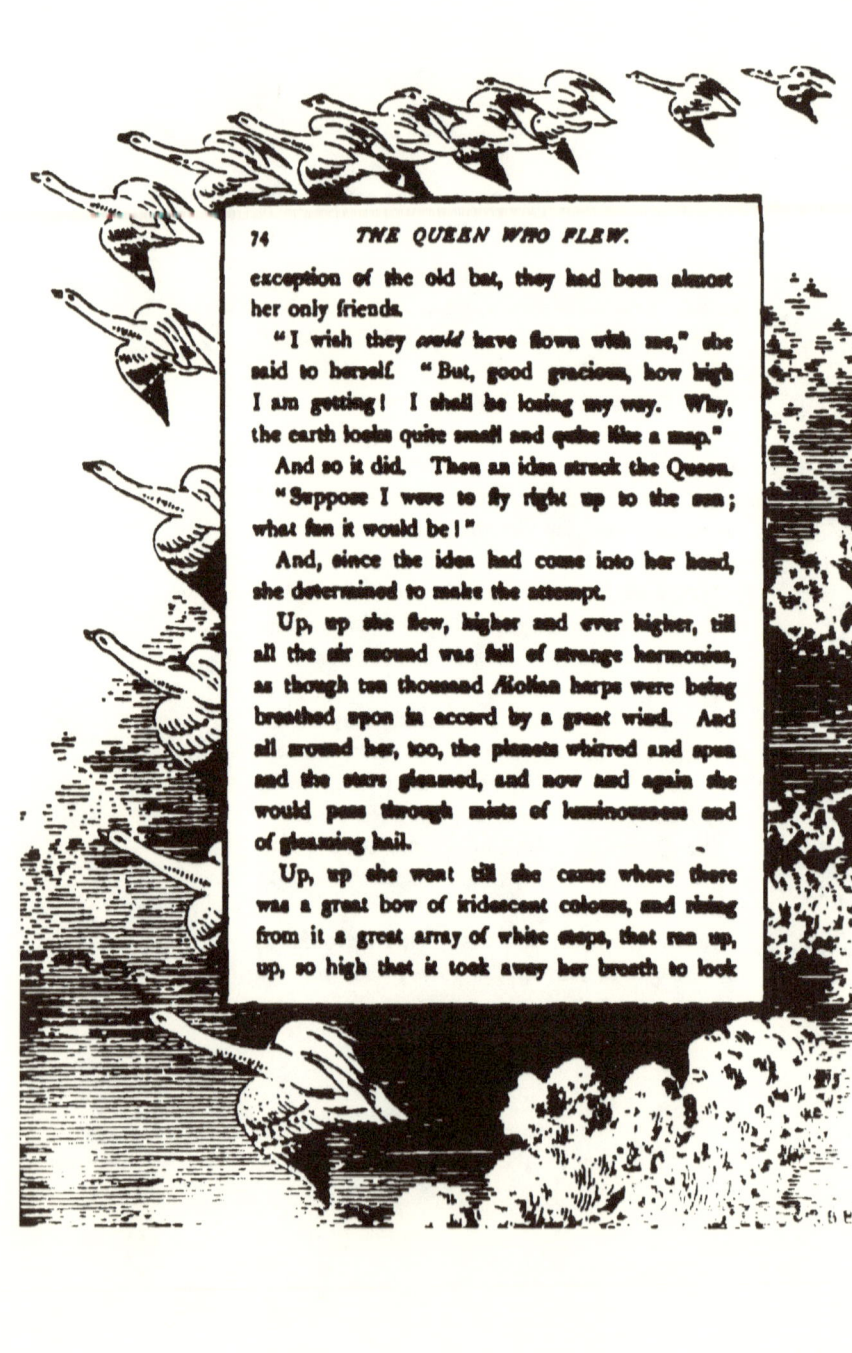

exception of the old bat, they had been almost
her only friends.

"I wish they *would* have flown with me," she
said to herself. "But, good gracious, how high
I am getting! I shall be losing my way. Why,
the earth looks quite small and quite like a map."

And so it did. Then an idea struck the Queen.

"Suppose I were to fly right up to the sun;
what fun it would be!"

And, since the idea had come into her head,
she determined to make the attempt.

Up, up she flew, higher and ever higher, till
all the air around was full of strange harmonies,
as though ten thousand Æolian harps were being
breathed upon in accord by a great wind. And
all around her, too, the planets whirred and spun
and the stars gleamed, and now and again she
would pass through mists of luminousness and
of gleaming hail.

Up, up she went till she came where there
was a great bow of iridescent colours, and rising
from it a great array of white steps, that ran up,
up, so high that it took away her breath to look

upon them. At the top was a great glare of light.

The Queen felt tired and a little bewildered; it seemed as if her wings would bear her no longer or, at least, no higher.

Upon the many-coloured road she stood and looked up the great white way. A voice spoke to her like a great rushing of wind.

"Maiden," it said, "so far and no further."

And a feeling akin to fear came over her; but not fear, for she knew not what guilt was.

And the voice spoke again. "Go down this bow back to the earth, and do the work that is to be done by you. Be of use to your fellows."

And the Queen turned and went her way down the great road. The air was full of voices, glad voices, such that the Queen had never heard before—full of a joy that made her heart leap to hear.

But she could see no one.

Till at last she came back to the green earth, late in the afternoon.

For a moment, above her, she could see the

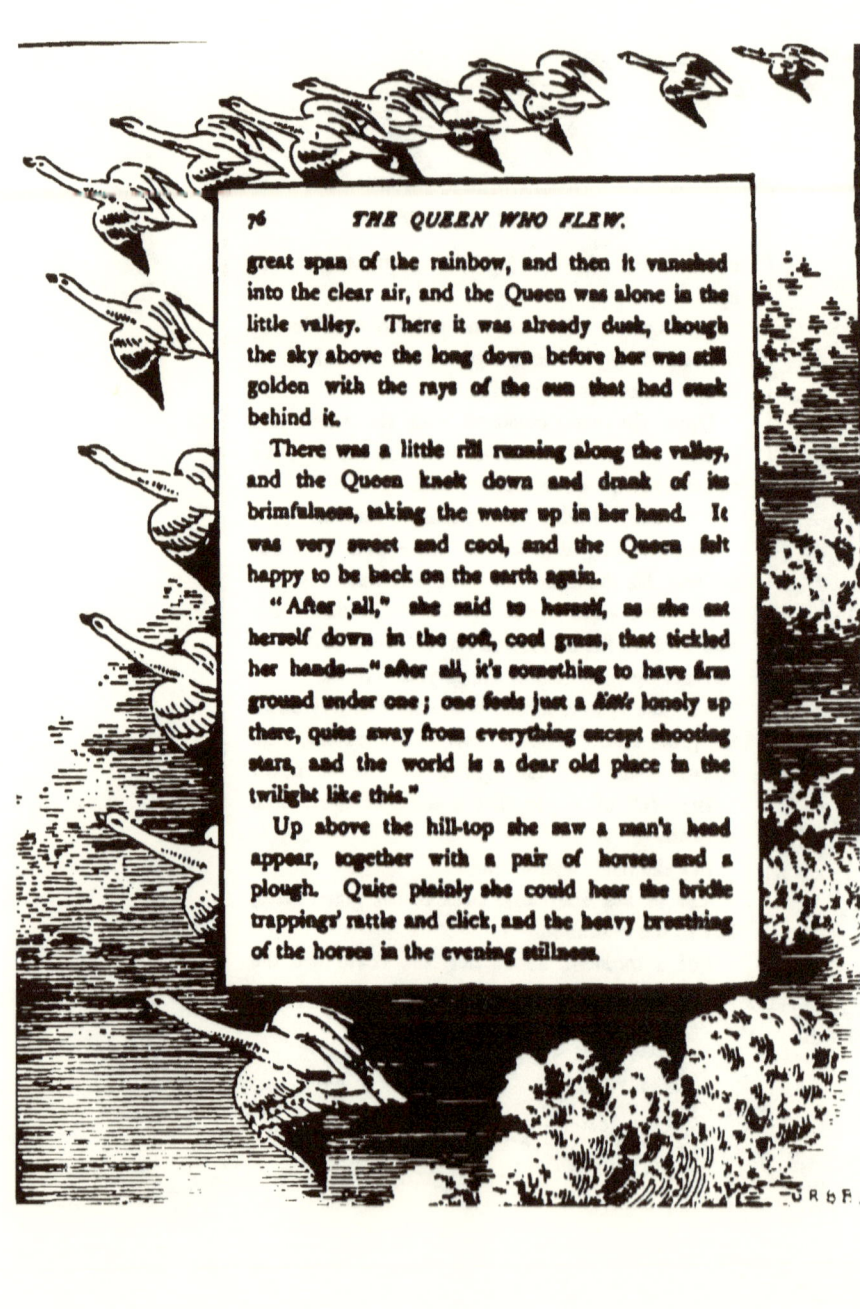

great span of the rainbow, and then it vanished into the clear air, and the Queen was alone in the little valley. There it was already dusk, though the sky above the long down before her was still golden with the rays of the sun that had sunk behind it.

There was a little rill running along the valley, and the Queen knelt down and drank of its brimfulness, taking the water up in her hand. It was very sweet and cool, and the Queen felt happy to be back on the earth again.

"After all," she said to herself, as she sat herself down in the soft, cool grass, that tickled her hands—"after all, it's something to have firm ground under one; one feels just a *little* lonely up there, quite away from everything except shooting stars, and the world is a dear old place in the twilight like this."

Up above the hill-top she saw a man's head appear, together with a pair of horses and a plough. Quite plainly she could hear the bridle trappings' rattle and click, and the heavy breathing of the horses in the evening stillness.

It was all so quiet and natural that she did not feel at all surprised.

Just at the brow of the hill, standing out black against the light, the man halted, and, lifting the plough, turned his team of horses round and set off down the new furrow.

With very little hesitation, the Queen went up the hill towards the spot from which he had disappeared, and in a very short time she had reached the brow and stood looking down the furrows. The western sky was still a blaze of glory, and the yellow light gleamed along the ridge of shining earth that the plough turned up, and on the steel of the ploughshare. The plough-man was singing a song, and his voice came mellowly along over the sunlit stubble that was not yet ploughed up.

" I wonder, now, if it will be safe for me to speak to him, or if he'll fall in love with me as soon as he sees me? because it's really too much of a nuisance."

However, she went lightly across the stubble towards him. He was just turning the plough

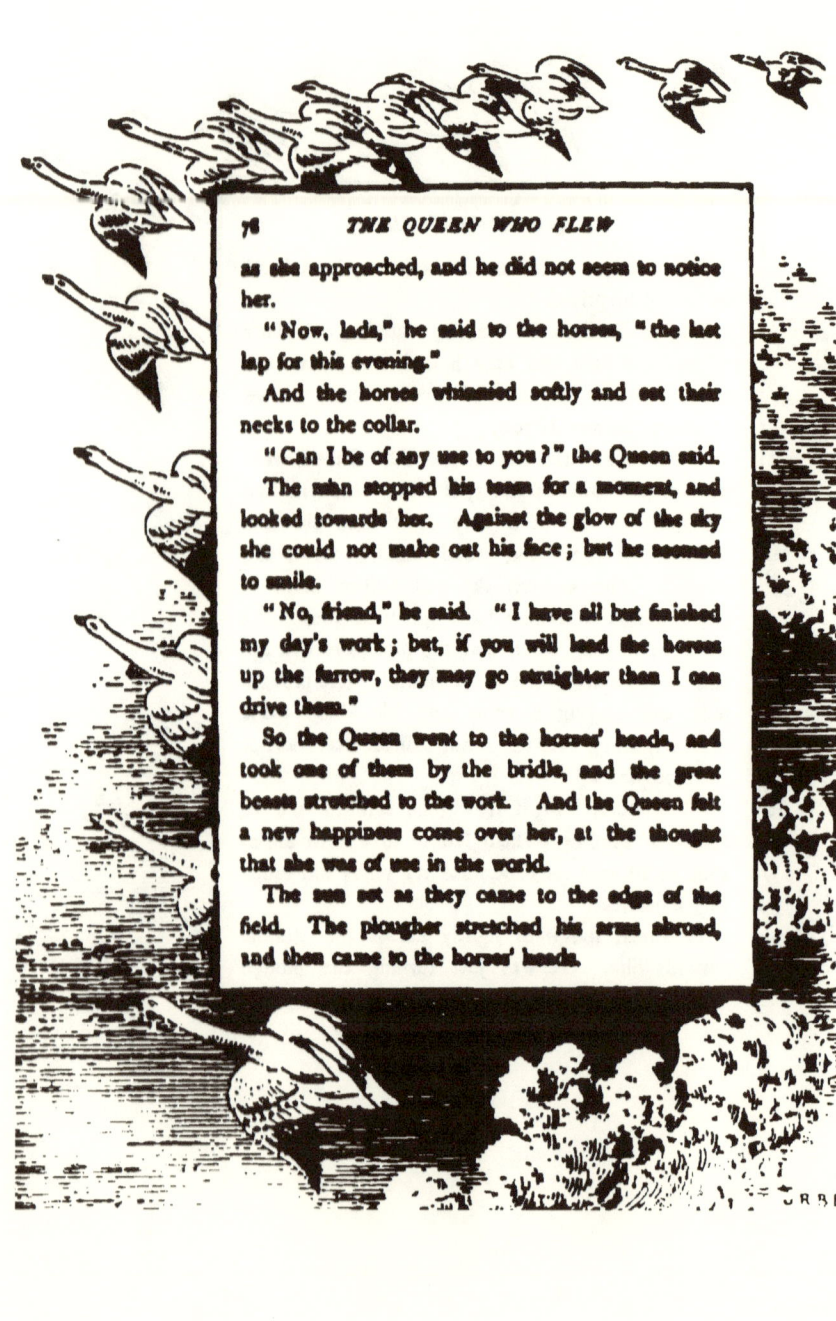

as she approached, and he did not seem to notice her.

"Now, lads," he said to the horses, "the last lap for this evening."

And the horses whinnied softly and set their necks to the collar.

"Can I be of any use to you?" the Queen said.

The man stopped his team for a moment, and looked towards her. Against the glow of the sky she could not make out his face; but he seemed to smile.

"No, friend," he said. "I have all but finished my day's work; but, if you will lead the horses up the furrow, they may go straighter than I can drive them."

So the Queen went to the horses' heads, and took one of them by the bridle, and the great beasts stretched to the work. And the Queen felt a new happiness come over her, at the thought that she was of use in the world.

The sun set as they came to the edge of the field. The plougher stretched his arms abroad, and then came to the horses' heads.

"Thank you, friend," he said to the Queen. He did not look at her, but kept his eyes downcast on the ground with a strangely distant appearance in them. "Will you not come home and sup with us? It is hardly a hundred yards to the farm, and the nearest place to here is several miles onwards."

The Queen said, "Thank you. I should be very glad; but—but—" as the thought struck her, "I shan't be able to pay you, you know."

The ploughman laughed. "Now I see you are a stranger," he said. "But yet I have seldom had strangers pass here that offered to help me."

The Queen said, "Yes, but it is so nice to be of use to any one;" and seeing that he was engaged in unbuckling the horse from the plough on the right side, she did as much for the one on the left.

The ploughman said, "Now, can you ride?"

"Well, I've never tried, but I dare say I could if they didn't go *too* fast."

"No, I don't think they'll go fast," he said.

"Here, let me lift you on.   There, catch hold of the horns of the collar."

And in a moment the Queen was seated sideways on the great horse. The ploughman made his way to the horse's head and led it down the valley again. The other horse went quietly along by the side of them.

"How delicious everything looks in the owl-light!" the Queen said.

And the ploughman sighed. "I—I can't see it," he said. "I can't see anything. I'm blind."

The Queen said, "Blind! Why, I should never have known it. You are as skilful as any one else."

The ploughman answered, "Oh yes, I can manage pretty well because I'm used to it, and there are many ways of managing things; but it is an affliction."

The horses went carefully down the hill, and in a little space they had reached the valley whence the Queen had started. It was now quite dark there, and the harvest moon had not yet arisen, but at no great distance from them the Queen could see a light winking.

So the horses plodded along, stopping now and
again to crop a mouthful of grass or drink a
draught from the tinkling rill, whose sound had
grown loud in the twilight silence. In a very short
while they had come to where a little farmhouse
lay in the bottom of the valley among trees, that
looked black in the starlight.

The ploughman called, "Mother, I'm bringing
a visitor."

And a little old woman came to the door.
"Welcome!" she said, and added, "My dear,"
when the Queen came into sight in the light that
fell through the open door.

The Queen slipped down from the horse and
went into the door with the little old woman, whilst
the ploughman disappeared with the horses.

"She really is a dear little old woman," the
Queen said to herself—"very different from old
Mrs. Hexer."

And so indeed she was—quite a little woman in
comparison with her stalwart son, with white hair
and a rosy face and eyes not at all age-dimmed,
but blue as the cornflower or as a summer sky,

G

and looking, like a child's, so gentle that a hard word would make them wince.

She put a chair ready for the Queen by the fireside, and then, on the white wood table, set out forks and knives for her.

"You must be tired," she said kindly; "but we go to bed soon after supper, and so you will have a good rest."

The Queen said, "Yes, I am a little tired; and it is very kind of you to let me stop."

The little old woman looked at her with an odd, amused look in her gentle eyes.

"Now I see you are a stranger," she said.

"Yes, I come from a long way off," the Queen said. "At least I suppose it is a great way off, for it has taken me a long time to get here."

At that moment the ploughman came in, with the heavy step of a tired man.

"Mother, mother!" he said gaily; "I'm hungry."

"Son, son," she answered, "I am glad to hear it. There will be plenty."

And so the supper was made ready, and heartily

glad the Queen was, for she was as hungry as the ploughman.

And they had the whitest of floury potatoes, in the whitest of white wooden bowls, and the sweetest of new milk, and the clearest of honey overrunning the comb, and junket laid on rushes, and plums, and apples, and apricots. And be certain that the Queen enjoyed it.

And, when it was finished, they drew their chairs round the fire, and the ploughman said, addressing the Queen—

"Now, friend, since you have travelled far, tell us something of what may have befallen you on the way, for we are such stay-at-home folk here, that we know little of the world around. But perhaps you are tired and would rather go to bed."

But the Queen said, "Oh no, I am very well rested now, and I will gladly tell you my story—only first tell me where I am."

"This is the farm of Woodward, from which we take our names, my mother and I, and we are some ten miles from the Narrow Seas."

"But what is the land called, and who rules it?" the Queen said.

The ploughman laughed. "Why, it is called the land of the Happy Folk; and as for who rules it, why, just nobody, because it gets along very well as it is."

The Queen leant back in the great chair they had given her. She rubbed her chin reflectively and looked at the fire.

"The Regent told me that a country couldn't possibly exist without a King or Queen," she said.

"Who is the Regent?" the ploughman said. He too kept his face to the fire that he could not see.

"Oh, well, he's just the Regent of my kingdom. But I forgot you didn't know. I am Eldrida, Queen of the Narrowlands and all the Isles."

The little old woman looked at her interestedly.

And the ploughman said, "After all, you're not so very far from your home; because one can see the coast of it quite plainly on a clear day from our shore, so they say."

"Why, then you must have quite a number of people from there?" the Queen said.

But the ploughman answered, "No, hardly ever any one, because the seas run so swiftly through the straights that no boat can live in them—so people would have to come a long way round by land. Besides, they've got everything that we've got, so what could they want here?" the ploughman said, and added slily, "all except one thing, that is."

"Why, what is that?" the Queen asked.

And the ploughman answered, "Why, the Queen, of course; because we have got her."

But the little old woman held her hand to shield her eyes from the fire's blaze, and looked across at the Queen.

"I shouldn't think it was a very nice country to live in," she said.

The Queen asked, "Why?"

"Well, one evening when we were down by the sea, we saw the whole sky lit up over there, and, later, we heard from a traveller, that the people had set fire to the town when they were fighting about who was to be Regent."

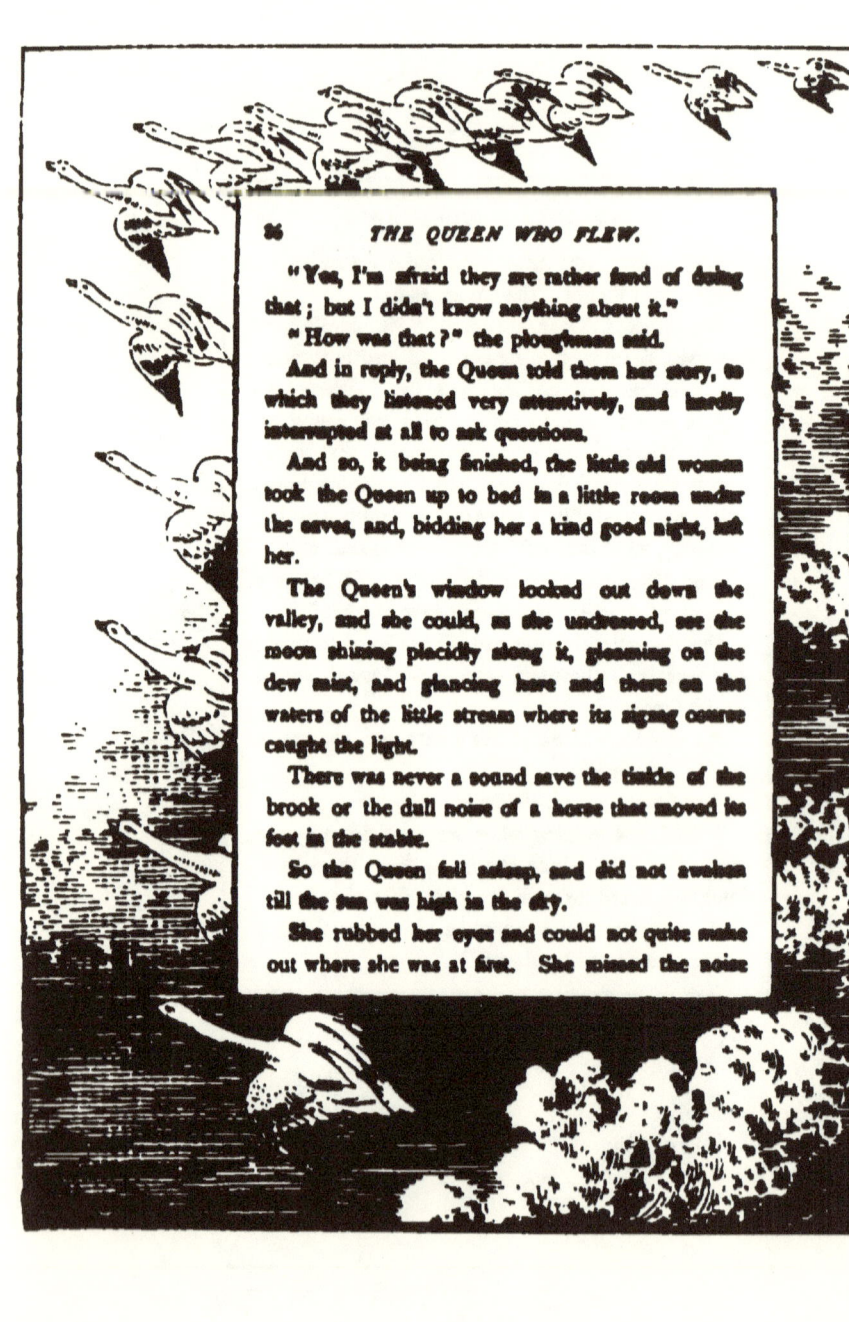

"Yes, I'm afraid they are rather fond of doing that; but I didn't know anything about it."

"How was that?" the ploughman said.

And in reply, the Queen told them her story, to which they listened very attentively, and hardly interrupted at all to ask questions.

And so, it being finished, the little old woman took the Queen up to bed in a little room under the eaves, and, bidding her a kind good night, left her.

The Queen's window looked out down the valley, and she could, as she undressed, see the moon shining placidly along it, gleaming on the dew mist, and glancing here and there on the waters of the little stream where its zigzag course caught the light.

There was never a sound save the tinkle of the brook or the dull noise of a horse that moved its feet in the stable.

So the Queen fell asleep, and did not awaken till the sun was high in the sky.

She rubbed her eyes and could not quite make out where she was at first. She missed the noise

of the geese, to which she had been used to awaken. But gradually it all came back to her, and for a while she lay and watched the roses that were peeping in at the window and nodding in the morning breeze.

"Come, this will never do!" the Queen said to herself. "Whatever will they think of me?" So she arose from between the warm, clean sheets, and, having dressed herself, went downstairs. There she found the little old woman busy in the kitchen.

"Good morning, my dear," she said.

And the Queen answered, "Good morning, mother."

And the little old woman's eyes smiled her pleasure. "I didn't wish to wake you," she said, "you seemed so tired last night. My son has gone off to his ploughing; but you will see him as you pass the hill, and he will guide you a little on your way, if you have to go further." The little old woman's eyes looked quite wistful. "We wish you would stay a little while with us; we should like it so much."

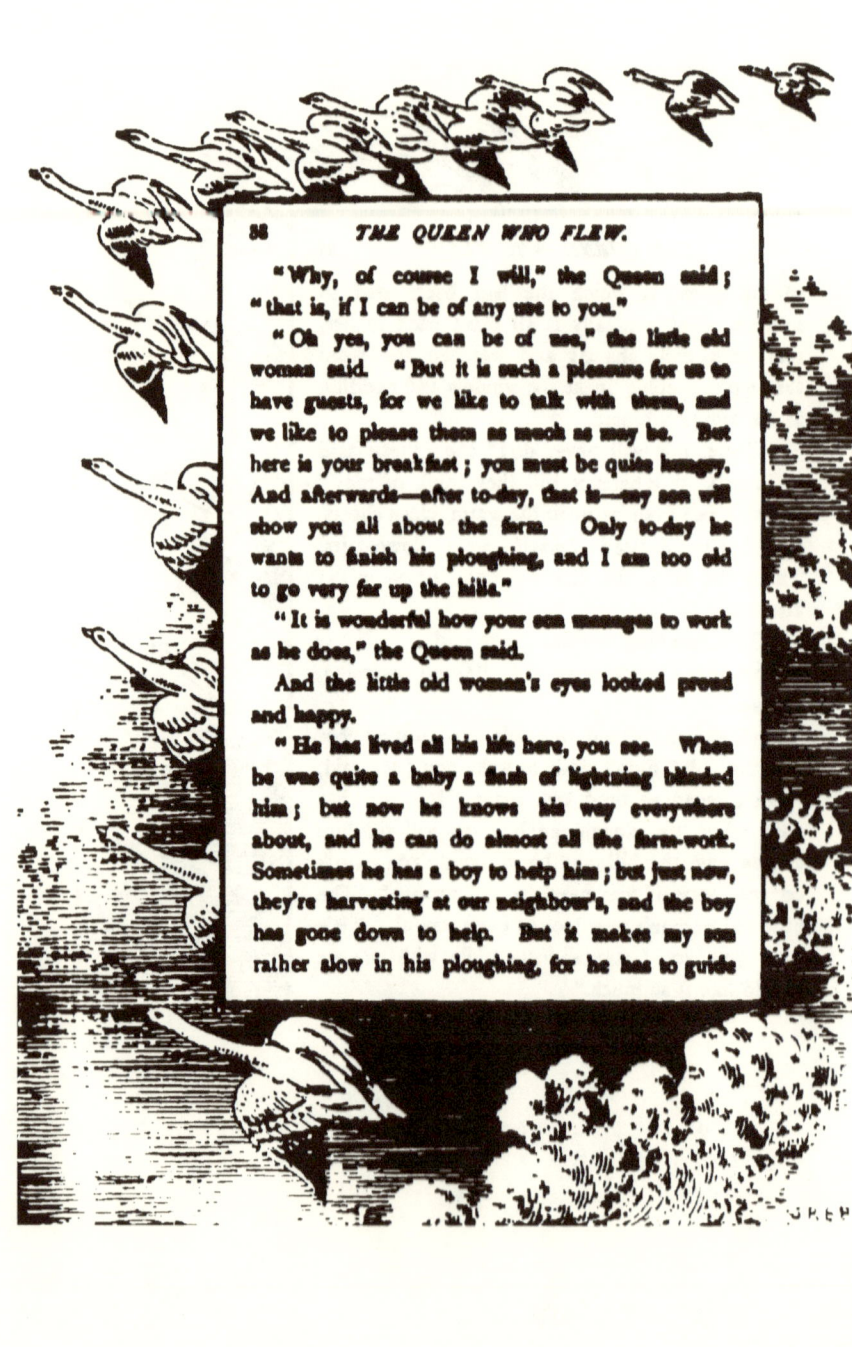

"Why, of course I will," the Queen said; "that is, if I can be of any use to you."

"Oh yes, you can be of use," the little old woman said. "But it is such a pleasure for us to have guests, for we like to talk with them, and we like to please them as much as may be. But here is your breakfast; you must be quite hungry. And afterwards—after to-day, that is—my son will show you all about the farm. Only to-day he wants to finish his ploughing, and I am too old to go very far up the hills."

"It is wonderful how your son manages to work as he does," the Queen said.

And the little old woman's eyes looked proud and happy.

"He has lived all his life here, you see. When he was quite a baby a flash of lightning blinded him; but now he knows his way everywhere about, and he can do almost all the farm-work. Sometimes he has a boy to help him; but just now, they're harvesting at our neighbour's, and the boy has gone down to help. But it makes my son rather slow in his ploughing, for he has to guide

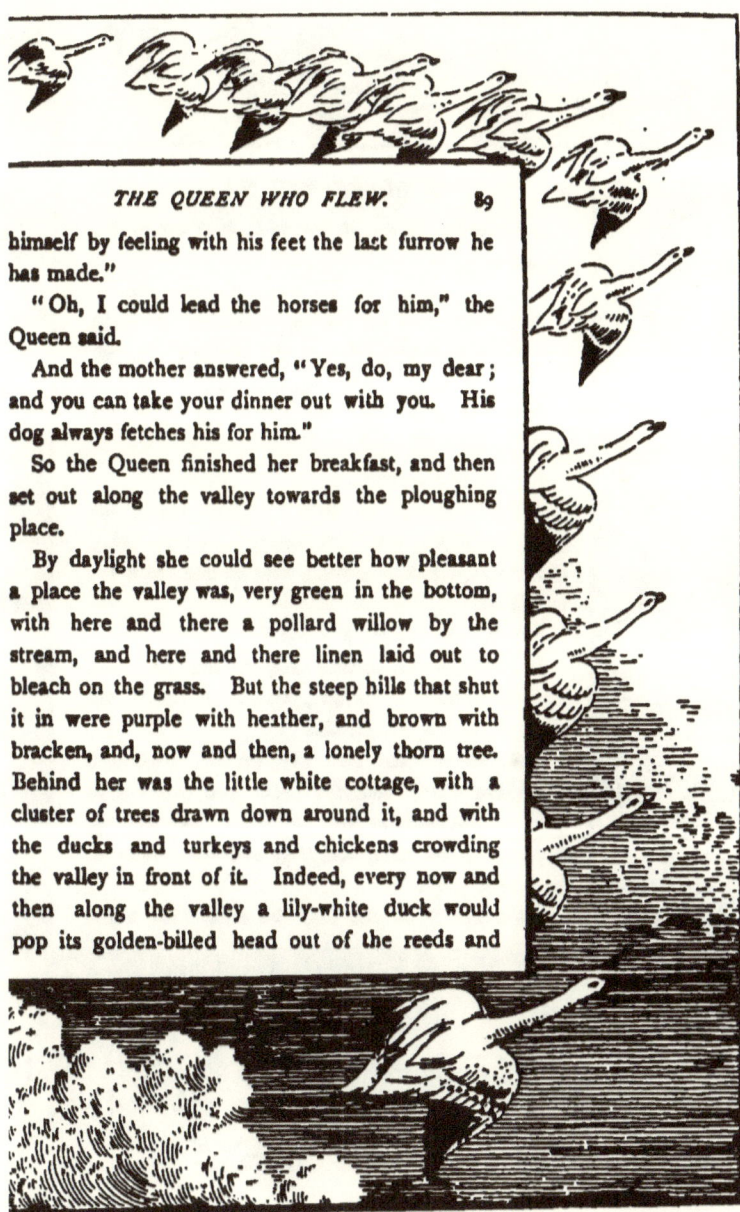

himself by feeling with his feet the last furrow he has made."

"Oh, I could lead the horses for him," the Queen said.

And the mother answered, "Yes, do, my dear; and you can take your dinner out with you. His dog always fetches his for him."

So the Queen finished her breakfast, and then set out along the valley towards the ploughing place.

By daylight she could see better how pleasant a place the valley was, very green in the bottom, with here and there a pollard willow by the stream, and here and there linen laid out to bleach on the grass. But the steep hills that shut it in were purple with heather, and brown with bracken, and, now and then, a lonely thorn tree. Behind her was the little white cottage, with a cluster of trees drawn down around it, and with the ducks and turkeys and chickens crowding the valley in front of it. Indeed, every now and then along the valley a lily-white duck would pop its golden-billed head out of the reeds and

meadow-sweet of the stream to look at her as she passed along.

So she came to the hill where the valley made a sharp turn, and on the top of which she could see the ploughman. Up it she climbed through the heather, and speedily reached him.

"I've come to lead the horses for you," she said.

And he looked towards her and smiled.

"That's right," he said. "Then you're not going away just yet. It's better here than being shut up in a palace garden, with no one but a but to talk to."

"It is," the Queen said simply.

So, through the autumn day, she led the horses up and down the furrows, whilst he drove the share deep into the ground.

And through the blue sky, up the wind and down the wind, came the crows and starlings to feed on the worms that the plough turned up. So, late in the afternoon, they had come as far as he meant to go.

"Further down the hill," he said, "the wheat

would catch the north wind. So that's enough for to-day, Queen Eldrida."

"Don't call me *Queen* Eldrida, because, if I am a queen, I'm not your queen. Just call me Eldrida."

"One name's as good as another," he said, as he slipped on his coat. "Now let's go home, and I'll show you a little of the valley behind the house."

So the Queen stayed for a while with them, and did as they did. And the blind man led her up the hills, and on the hilltops called the sheep, and from all sides they came to his call.

And the Queen halved his work for him, and did those things which his want of sight prevented his doing.

Sometimes she stayed to help the little mother indoors, but, on the whole, she preferred being out in the open air with the blind man.

Then came the beginning of winter, and she went with him up the hillsides, and in among the storms to fold the sheep, and drive the cattle home to the byres.

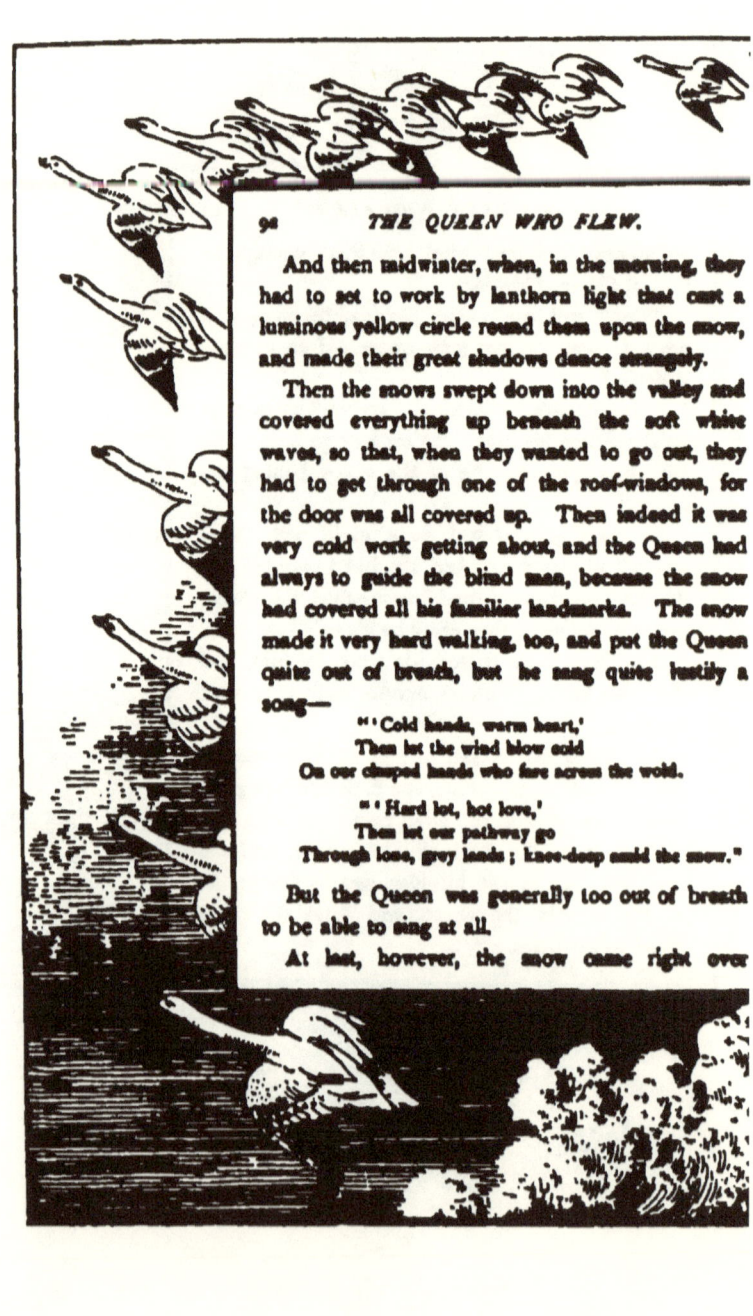

And then midwinter, when, in the morning, they had to set to work by lanthorn light that cast a luminous yellow circle round them upon the snow, and made their great shadows dance strangely.

Then the snows swept down into the valley and covered everything up beneath the soft white waves, so that, when they wanted to go out, they had to get through one of the roof-windows, for the door was all covered up. Then indeed it was very cold work getting about, and the Queen had always to guide the blind man, because the snow had covered all his familiar landmarks. The snow made it very hard walking, too, and put the Queen quite out of breath, but he sang quite lustily a song—

    "'Cold hands, warm heart,'
      Then let the wind blow cold
  On our clasped hands who fare across the wold.

     "'Hard lot, hot love,'
      Then let our pathway go
  Through lone, grey lands; knee-deep amid the snow."

But the Queen was generally too out of breath to be able to sing at all.

At last, however, the snow came right over

fire, and the little old woman span, and the Queen
worked at the loom, and the blind man wove
baskets out of osiers. And they told tales.

Said the little old woman, "I will tell you a
tale that I had from my grandmother, and she
had it from hers, and so on, a great way back.

"Once upon a time, upon the earth there were
no people at all, no men and women, but only
little goblin things that covered the whole earth
and made it a beautiful green colour. But the
sun was a bright flame colour, and the moon very,
very white. So the Sun and the Earth took to
quarrelling as to which was the more beautiful of
the two.

"Said the Earth, 'I am the more beautiful;
such a lovely green as mine was surely never
seen.'

"Said the Sun, 'But just look at my mantle
of flame.'

"So, as they could not possibly agree, they
submitted the matter to the Moon. Now, the

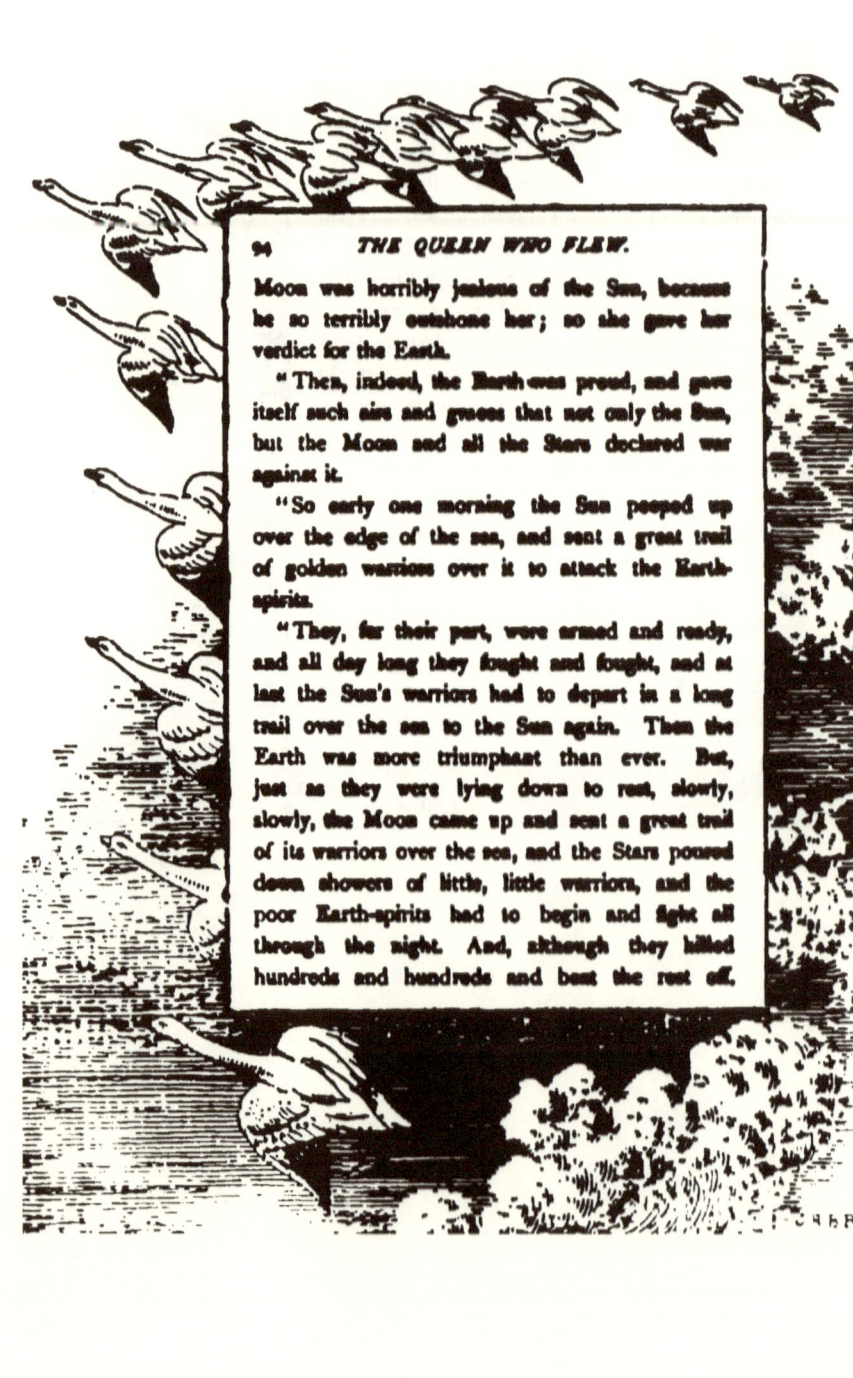

Moon was horribly jealous of the Sun, because he so terribly outshone her; so she gave her verdict for the Earth.

"Then, indeed, the Earth was proud, and gave itself such airs and graces that not only the Sun, but the Moon and all the Stars declared war against it.

"So early one morning the Sun peeped up over the edge of the sea, and sent a great trail of golden warriors over it to attack the Earth-spirits.

"They, for their part, were armed and ready, and all day long they fought and fought, and at last the Sun's warriors had to depart in a long trail over the sea to the Sun again. Then the Earth was more triumphant than ever. But, just as they were lying down to rest, slowly, slowly, the Moon came up and sent a great trail of its warriors over the sea, and the Stars poured down showers of little, little warriors, and the poor Earth-spirits had to begin and fight all through the night. And, although they killed hundreds and hundreds and beat the rest off,

no sooner was it done than they had to begin all over again against the Sun.

"This went on—day in, day out ; night in, night out—for a long, long time, until the poor Earth-spirits grew wearier and wearier, and their lovely green colour changed into a sickly yellow hue.

"Then in despair they prayed to the spirits of the air and of the great waters to assist them. And the waters arose and covered in the Earth, and the winds of the air brought a mantle of clouds, so that the Earth was shielded from the fury of the Sun and the constellations ; but, alas ! when the waters receded and the skies grew clear again, it was found that all the poor Earth-spirits were drowned — all save a very few who had taken refuge on the tops of the mountains.

"So these few, having such a lot to eat, gradually grew and grew till they became men. And the dead bodies of the green Earth-spirits grew out of the Earth, too, and became the fruits of the Earth ; but the dead bodies of the Sun and Moon warriors became gold and silver, and men dig them out of the Earth.

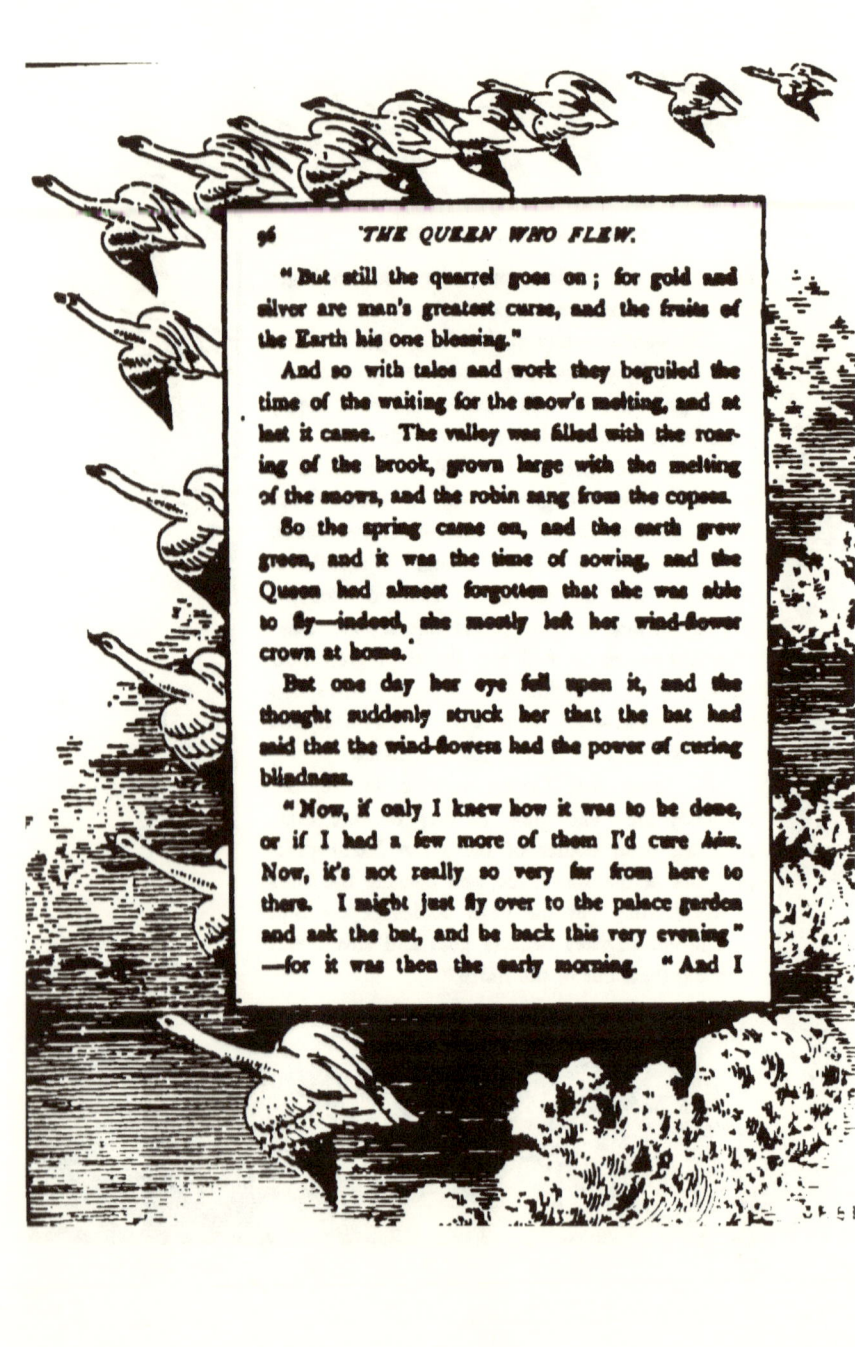

"But still the quarrel goes on; for gold and silver are man's greatest curse, and the fruits of the Earth his one blessing."

And so with tales and work they beguiled the time of the waiting for the snow's melting, and at last it came. The valley was filled with the roaring of the brook, grown large with the melting of the snows, and the robin sang from the copses.

So the spring came on, and the earth grew green, and it was the time of sowing, and the Queen had almost forgotten that she was able to fly—indeed, she mostly left her wind-flower crown at home.

But one day her eye fell upon it, and the thought suddenly struck her that the bat had said that the wind-flowers had the power of curing blindness.

"Now, if only I knew how it was to be done, or if I had a few more of them I'd cure *him*. Now, it's not really so very far from here to there. I might just fly over to the palace garden and ask the bat, and be back this very evening"—for it was then the early morning. "And I

won't tell them anything about it, and it'll be delightful."

And so, without any more hesitation, she just opened the little window and was up among the dawn-clouds that were sweeping up from over the sea. It was a little chilly and very lonely up there, and the silent flights of seagulls that she caught up and overpassed seemed too alarmed to talk to her. The Queen felt a little lost, as if there were something missing.

"Somehow it doesn't seem half as nice as it used to do," she said to herself. "I wonder why it is? I don't think, after I get home—I mean back here—I shall ever go flying again."

But she folded her hands in her cloak and went silently on over the grey shimmering sea. The sun grew higher and higher, and it was about eight in the morning before she was hovering over the city.

She alighted in a street that seemed somewhat empty, because she disliked the attention that her mode of progression usually excited.

Just in front of her, under a shed formed by

H

the pushing up of the shutters of his shop, a tailor was seated, cross-legged, working away with his head bent down over his work.

"Good morning!" the Queen said. "Can I be of any use to you?"

The tailor peered up at her through a great pair of horn spectacles.

"Eh?" he said.

"I said, 'Can I be of any use to you?'" the Queen replied.

And the tailor regarded her in a dazed way. Suddenly he said—

"Oh yes; marry me, marry me, only marry me!"

The Queen said, "Oh, nonsense," because she had just remembered the elixir.

But the tailor answered, "It isn't nonsense—it really isn't. It's true I'm married already; but I'll knock my wife on the head, and then I'll be free."

But before the Queen could answer anything at all there began a sudden growling sound that resolved itself into a succession of footsteps coming

rapidly down wooden steps, and, in, a moment, a door burst open just behind the tailor's back. There was an old woman with a great broom just behind it.

"Ah, would ye now! murder your wife, a respectable married woman, for the sake of a hussy that comes dropping down out of the chimney-tops. I'll teach you."

And with one sweep of her broom she knocked the poor little tailor off his board, and made a dash at the Queen.

But the Queen took to her heels and ran off.

"Why, she's worse than Mrs. Hexer," she said to herself. "But really this elixir is a great nuisance. It makes it impossible to have any peace. But I wonder what all the flags and decorations are about."

Just at that moment two people, who appeared to be a servant-girl and her mother, came out of a neighbouring house. They were very gay in holiday costume.

"What is to happen to-day?" the Queen asked. And the mother answered, "Why, don't you

know? The Queen is twenty-one to-day, and she's going to marry the Regent, Lord Blackjowl."

"Going to marry the Regent!" the Queen said. "Why, who told you so?"

"Everybody knows it," the mother answered.

"But how did everybody get to know it?" the Queen asked.

And the mother answered, "The Regent told them, I suppose."

And the girl said, "It's up among the Royal proclamations, on the notice-board at the palace."

The Queen said, "Oh! Will you show me the way to the palace?" she continued.

"Why, certainly," the girl said. "We were just going that way to see the procession."

So they set off through the gay streets. As they went along the Queen could see the young men on every side falling in love with her; but she paid no attention to them.

"Are you glad the Queen's going to be married?" she asked her guides.

And the girl answered, "Oh yes; we get a holiday to go and see the procession."

"Why, then, I suppose you'd be just as glad if the Queen died, and you could go and see her funeral?"

And the old woman said, "Of course!"

By that time they had come to the market-place. It was crowded with those who had come to see the sights, and the fountains were running wine instead of water; so, of course, there was rather a scramble to get at the fountains. That left the ground clear for the Queen to get to the notice-board where the Royal Proclamation hung.

There she saw, sure enough, the Regent's proclamation, saying that the Queen would marry him that day. At the end of it there was the signature, "*Eldrida, Queen.*"

"Why, it isn't my signature at all," the Queen said.

And the mother and daughter looked at her askance.

"Have any of you ever seen the Queen?" she asked.

And the mother answered, "No; no one has ever seen the Queen but the Regent; but there

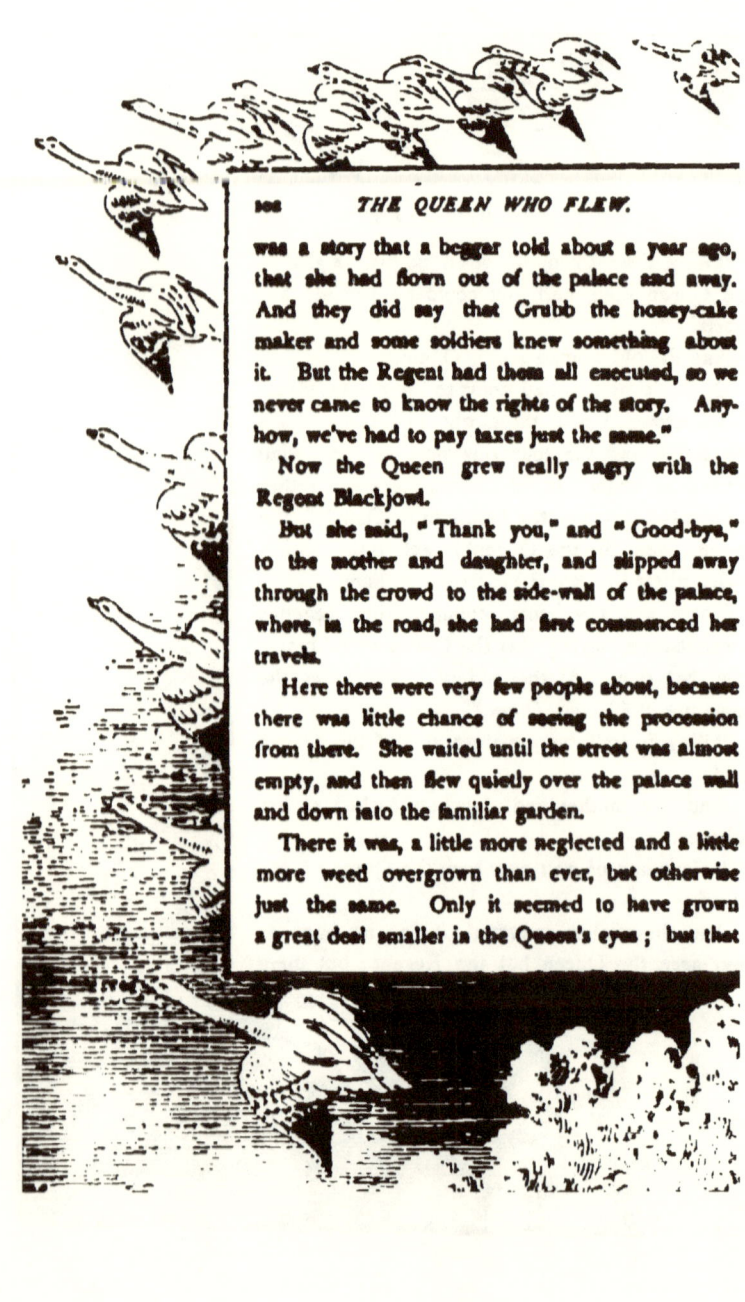

was a story that a beggar told about a year ago,
that she had flown out of the palace and away.
And they did say that Grubb the honey-cake
maker and some soldiers knew something about
it. But the Regent had them all executed, so we
never came to know the rights of the story. Anyhow, we've had to pay taxes just the same."

Now the Queen grew really angry with the
Regent Blackjowl.

But she said, " Thank you," and " Good-bye,"
to the mother and daughter, and slipped away
through the crowd to the side-wall of the palace,
where, in the road, she had first commenced her
travels.

Here there were very few people about, because
there was little chance of seeing the procession
from there. She waited until the street was almost
empty, and then flew quietly over the palace wall
and down into the familiar garden.

There it was, a little more neglected and a little
more weed overgrown than ever, but otherwise
just the same. Only it seemed to have grown
a great deal smaller in the Queen's eyes ; but that

was because she had grown accustomed to great prospects and wide expanses of country.

The long, thorny arms of the roses had grown so much, that it was quite difficult to get under them into the little seat.

"Now I shall have ever so much trouble to wake him, and he'll be fearfully surly," the Queen said to herself.

But it is always the unexpected that happens—as you will one day learn—and the Queen found that the rustling that the leaves made at her entrance had awakened the bat.

"Hullo!" he said, "you there! Glad to see you. Heard from a nightingale that you'd been seen in disreputable company, going about with geese. Well, and what did you think of the world?"

"Oh, it's a very nice place when you're used to it."

"That's what *you* think," the bat said. "Wait till you come to be my age. But now, tell me your adventures."

"I'd better humour him," the Queen said to herself, and so she plunged into the recital.

When she had finished the bat said, " H'm ! and so you're going to marry the Regent ? "

" I'm not going to do anything of the sort," the Queen said.

And the bat asked, " Who are you going to marry, then ? "

The Queen answered, " No one; at least—— "

And the bat said, " Just so."

And the Queen replied, " Don't be stupid. Oh, and tell me how one can cure blindness with wind-flowers."

The bat said, " Do you know how to make tea ? "

" Of course I do," the Queen answered.

" Well, you make an infusion of dried wind-flowers just like tea, and then you give it to the young scamp to drink."

" He's not a scamp," the Queen said; " but you're a dear good old bat all the same."

The bat said, " H'm ! "

The Queen rose to her feet. " Well, I must be off," she said. " I've got a lot to do."

The bat said, " Wait a minute; I'm coming too;" and he dropped down and hung on to

the Queen's shoulder. He was rather a weight, but the Queen suffered it.

"Why, there aren't any wind-flowers left!" the Queen said, surveying the spot where they had grown.

The bat said, "No; the weeds have choked them all."

The Queen rubbed her chin and said nothing.

And the bat merely ejaculated, "H'm!"

So the Queen entered the palace.

All the great halls were silent, and empty of people, and she passed through one after the other, shivering a little at their vastness.

At last she came before the curtain that separated her from the Throne Hall. It was large enough to contain the whole nation.

She pushed the curtain aside and found herself standing behind the great throne. Through the interstices of the carved back she could see everything that was going on. The Great Hall was thronged full of people from end to end. On the throne platform the Regent was waiting, evidently about to begin a speech.

The Queen stopped and peeped; there was a great flourish of trumpets that echoed and echoed along the hall, and the Regent began.

"Ladies noble, my lords, dames commoner, and gentlemen!" His great voice sounded clearly through the silence. "As you are well aware, our gracious and high-mighty sovereign, the Queen Eldrida, has deigned to favour my unworthy self with the priceless honour of her hand, and that on this auspicious day. Her hand and seal affixed to the weighty document you have seen in the market-place."

The Queen walked round the opposite side of the throne into the view of the people, who set up a tumultuous cheer. The Regent, however, thought they were cheering him, and went on with his speech.

"I had also announced that it was her Majesty's royal pleasure to reveal herself to her loyal people's eyes on this day."

The Queen slowly ascended the steps of the throne and seated herself thereon. The great gold crown—it was six feet high, and so heavy

The people cheered again, and still the Regent, whose back was to the throne, deemed that they were applauding his speech. He ran his fingers through his black beard and continued—

"It is, however, my painful duty to apprise you that her Majesty has been pleased to alter her design. We shall, therefore, be married in private in the Queen's apartments. The Queen's maiden modesty will not allow her to reveal her charms to the vulgar multitude."

He paused and watched the effect of his speech, nervously fingering his beard and blinking with his little eyes. The people whispered among themselves, evidently unable to understand what it meant.

Suddenly the Queen's voice rang through the hall.

"My people," she said, "it is an infamous lie! I am here."

The Regent started and turned round ; his face grew as pale as death. But from the people a

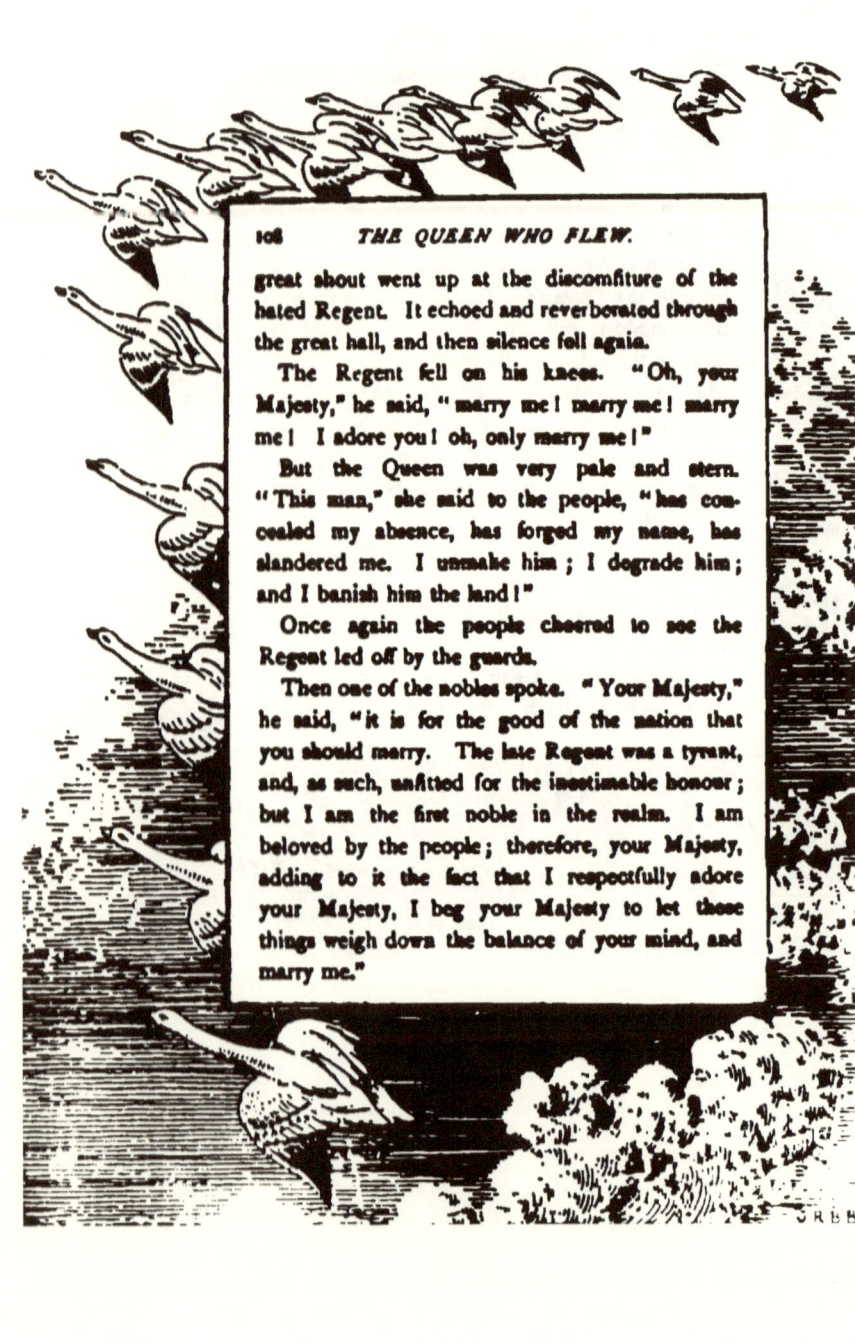

great shout went up at the discomfiture of the hated Regent. It echoed and reverberated through the great hall, and then silence fell again.

The Regent fell on his knees. "Oh, your Majesty," he said, "marry me! marry me! marry me! I adore you! oh, only marry me!"

But the Queen was very pale and stern. "This man," she said to the people, "has concealed my absence, has forged my name, has slandered me. I unmake him; I degrade him; and I banish him the land!"

Once again the people cheered to see the Regent led off by the guards.

Then one of the nobles spoke. "Your Majesty," he said, "it is for the good of the nation that you should marry. The late Regent was a tyrant, and, as such, unfitted for the inestimable honour; but I am the first noble in the realm. I am beloved by the people; therefore, your Majesty, adding to it the fact that I respectfully adore your Majesty, I beg your Majesty to let these things weigh down the balance of your mind, and marry me."

But hardly were the words out of his mouth when a tumult arose, the like of which was never heard in any land, for every man of the nation was shouting, "Marry me! marry me!" till the whole building quivered.

The Queen held up her hand for silence. "Listen!" she said. "I shall marry no one of you; and I will not even remain your Queen. For I am quite unfitted for a ruler, and I don't in the least want to be one. Therefore, choose a ruler for yourselves."

But the people with one voice shouted, "Be you our ruler!"

The Queen, however, said, "No; I cannot and will not. It wouldn't be any good at all; besides, all the men would love me a great deal too much, and all the women would hate me a great deal too much, because of their husbands and sweethearts and all. So you must choose a king for yourselves."

But confusion became doubly confounded, for every man in that vast assembly voted for himself as king.

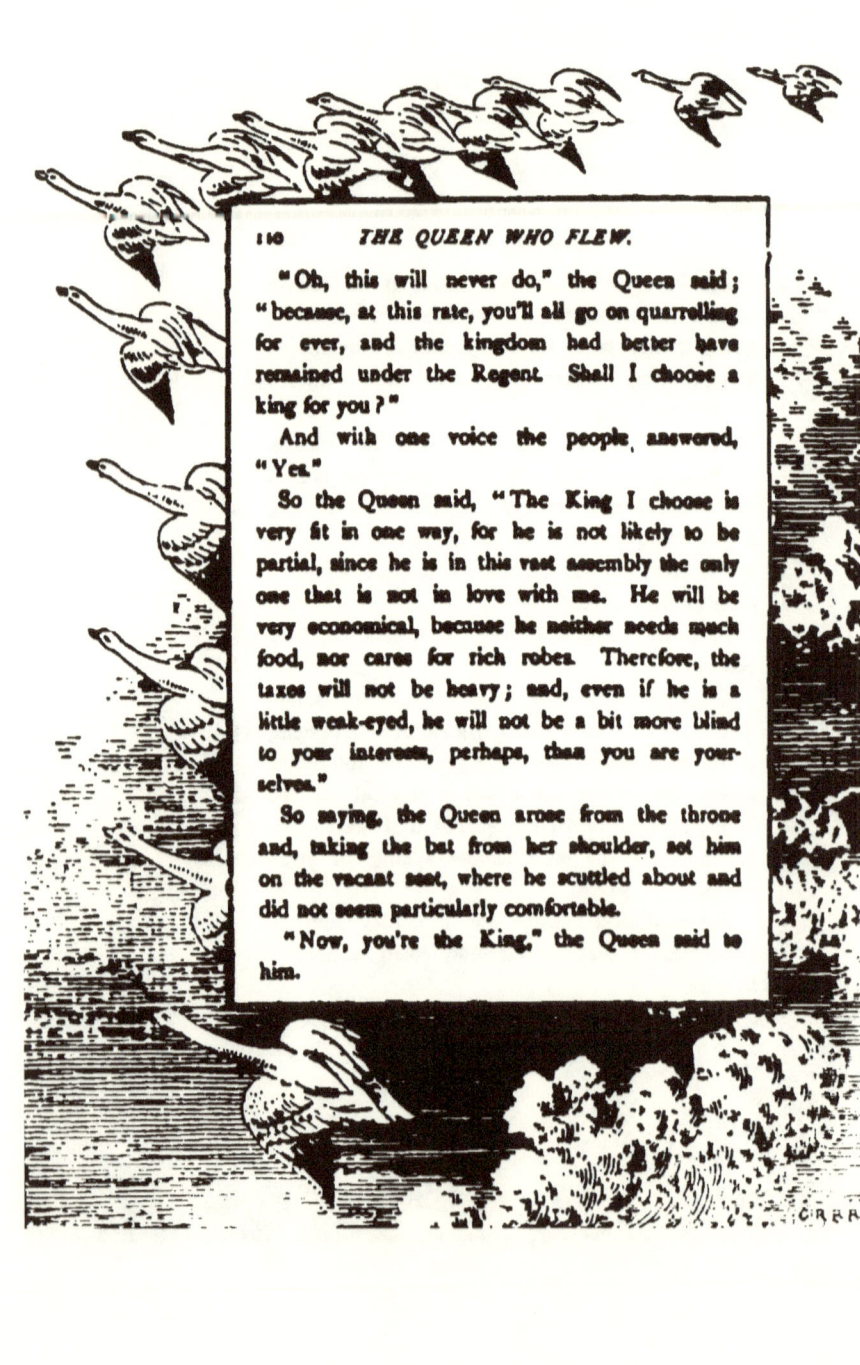

"Oh, this will never do," the Queen said; "because, at this rate, you'll all go on quarrelling for ever, and the kingdom had better have remained under the Regent. Shall I choose a king for you?"

And with one voice the people answered, "Yes."

So the Queen said, "The King I choose is very fit in one way, for he is not likely to be partial, since he is in this vast assembly the only one that is not in love with me. He will be very economical, because he neither needs much food, nor cares for rich robes. Therefore, the taxes will not be heavy; and, even if he is a little weak-eyed, he will not be a bit more blind to your interests, perhaps, than you are yourselves."

So saying, the Queen arose from the throne and, taking the bat from her shoulder, set him on the vacant seat, where he scuttled about and did not seem particularly comfortable.

"Now, you're the King," the Queen said to him.

"H'm!" he said. "Will they give me some raw meat?"

The Queen said, "Oh yes; and anything else you like to ask for."

The bat said, "H'm! this seat isn't very comfortable. What's that thing up there?"

"That's the crown," the Queen said.

And the King remarked, "H'm!" and in a moment he was hanging upside down from the bottom of the crown.

And the people cheered their King.

But the Queen just said, "Good-bye, your Majesty."

"Good-bye," the Bat said. "I suppose you won't marry *me*?"

"Don't be silly," the late Queen said; and she slipped behind the curtain and ran through the deserted halls again, and once more out into the garden. And once again she watered her favourite plants, for the last time, and then flew right up into the air and away, away over the troubled seas, to the land that lay low in the horizon.

"How delightful it feels not to be a Queen any

longer!" she said to herself. " I always used to feel afraid, when I sat under that great crown, that it might fall on my head and squash me altogether. But I wonder how the bat got on."

That the Queen never knew; but this was what happened. The bat took to kingship quite as easily as a duck takes to water, and, for reasons that the Queen gave, made a most popular ruler—even though he *was* strictly just. True, there were only three people in the kingdom who understood him, and they were mouse-trap makers who had learnt the bat language from mice. But, as the King always superintended the carrying out of his own edicts, they did not care to play tricks. And the Bat language was taught in all the schools, so that it became the state tongue. And all the ladies took to wearing brown sealskin cloaks with great puffed sleeves and capes, so as to look as much like bats as possible, and they all pretended to be very weak-sighted and turned night into day, in imitation of the King.

So that altogether the King was a great success from every point of view, as he was very long-

lived, the last news that has reached here from the Narrowlands, reported that his Majesty was still hanging head downwards from the great crown, and was still setting the fashion throughout the kingdom, though the news does not tell us that his people have yet resorted to hanging from the chandeliers by their toes.

But the Narrowlands is very far away from here, so that news does not often reach us from it; there is even no talk of opening the country up, which alone shows how difficult it must be to reach.

*　　*　　*　　*　　*

In the mean while the Queen had come to the other shore. She flew straight to the little cottage in the valley, and the cock who was standing on the doorsill greeted her with a lusty crow, being glad to see her again.

In the house there was no one to be found.

"The little mother must have gone to her bleaching," the Queen said to herself, "and he—oh, he told me he was going to work in the wood to-day, so now I'll see about making the infusion. The kettle's on the boil, and it won't take long."

I

She took off the faded wind-flower crown, and looked at it for a moment.

" You poor thing ! " she said, " it seems a shame, but still it can't be helped," and in a moment she had dropped it into the boiling water, which rapidly assumed the golden straw colour of a weak cup of tea. This she poured into a drinking-horn, and then set off with it into the wood at the back of the house. It was rather a ticklish task, walking through the low, dusky wood with the horn in her hand, for it was getting on in the day and the light was bad, and the small trees of which the wood was composed were difficult to walk among.

By her side the stream rushed and rustled over its rocky bottom, and her feet crackled too on the flooring of last year's fallen leaves, but the sound that she paused every now and then to listen for she could not hear. There came no sharp ringing of the axe down the valley among the trees.

" He must be binding the faggots together," she said to herself, and went on until she came to the clearing where he should have been at work ; but there he was not.

The light came down the valley duskily through the mist; it gleamed upon the stream and glimmered on the white ends of the newly chopped faggots that were neatly bound together with withies.

"He must have gone further on," she said to herself, and ran quite swiftly up the steep path that climbed into the heart of the mountains. The falling of the night frightened her a little, and she was anxious to find him.

Up and up the rocky path went, whilst the stream foamed down beside it, and at last she saw him in a slant of light that came down a west-facing valley. He was crossing the stream just above where it thundered over a great boulder.

There was a bridge across the torrent, but it was only a tree-trunk, and he preferred, in his blindness, to cross on the stream bottom, over the boulders with the aid of a good staff. The water foamed up to his knees.

She came as close to the water's edge as she could, and called—

"Why, where are you going to?"

In spite of the roaring of the waters he heard her and turned.

"Who are you?" he asked.

And she answered, "I am Eldrida."

And in a moment, with a great splashing of the black water, he was at her side.

"I thought you had gone for good," he said. "And so I worked as long as I felt able to; but just now it was all so silent and so dreadfully lonely, that I could not stand it, and I was about to set out to search for you through the world."

"What all alone, and blind?" she said.

And he answered, "Yes, since you were gone I was alone and blind; but if I had found you I should not have been alone, and hardly blind at all."

She put the horn into his hand, and said, "Drink this."

"Why, what is it?" she asked.

"It is what I went to fetch," she said; "drink it and see."

The light was shining on his face as he raised it to his mouth and drank it off, and suddenly there came into his eyes a look of great joy.

"Why," he said, "I can see!" and in a moment he had thrown his arms round her and drew her tightly to him. "I love you more than all the world!" he said. "Do you love me?"

She seemed to have forgotten all about the elixir, for instead of saying, "Don't be ridiculous!" she just said, "Yes, I love you very much."

And the stream roared on over the great boulder and whirled back over the rocky shallows, and the shadows in the valleys grew darker and darker; but they both had a great deal to say, though, as a matter of fact, it might most of it have been said with three words and a kiss.

But, you see, they preferred to do it in another way; at least, as far as the speaking went—in my experience, there is only one way of kissing.

"So you see, I shan't be able to fly away any more," she said, after she had related her story, "because the poor wind-flower crown is all boiled."

"Oh, well," he said, "I dare say you won't want it again, unless you get very tired of me."

And she said, "Don't be ridiculous!" but even that had nothing to do with the elixir.

And so they went home down the dark valley to the cottage.

The little mother smiled to see Eldrida.

"I knew you would come back," she said; "but my son was in a dreadful state—weren't you, son, son?"

And he only answered, "Mother, mother, I was. And I am very hungry; and I can see again!"

So there was great rejoicing in the cottage that night, and the little old woman's eyes grew bright with joy-tears.

But next day Eldrida and her love were married, and, from that time forth, they worked together, and went hand in hand up the tranquil valley or in among the storms on the hillcrests, and so lived happily ever after.

THE END.

PRINTED BY WILLIAM CLOWES AND SONS, LIMITED,
LONDON AND BECCLES.

CHILDREN'S BOOKS.

NURSERY LYRICS.

By Mrs. RICHARD STRACHEY.

ILLUSTRATED BY G. P. JACOMB HOOD.

Imperial 16mo. Price 3s. 6d.

An alphabet designed by the artist is inserted in the volume so that the donor may cut out the child's initials and fix them in the spaces provided on the cover.

"Pretty quaint nursery rhymes. . . . Sweet and simple."—*St. James's Budget.*

"A funny little excellent book for children is this. . . . Will delight the small folks by day, and send them happily to bed at night."—*Black and White.*

"Will certainly haunt childish heads."—*Graphic.*

"Merry jingles."—*Times.*

THE ADVENTURES OF PRINCE ALMERO.

By WILHELMINA PICKERING.

ILLUSTRATED BY MARGARET HOOPER.

Second Edition. Fcap. 4to. Cloth Extra. Price 3s. 6d.

Opinion of the Press on the First Edition.

"An original and charming tale of the fairies of the sea, told with much grace, and riveting our interest throughout. The Author, in her preface, makes modest apologies for appearing in print; but no apology, indeed, is needed, and we shall hope to see more of her work."—*Athenæum, November 29, 1890.*

HERCULES AND THE MARIONETTES.

By R. MURRAY GILCHRIST.

ILLUSTRATED BY C. P. SAINTON.

Fcap. 4to. 5s.